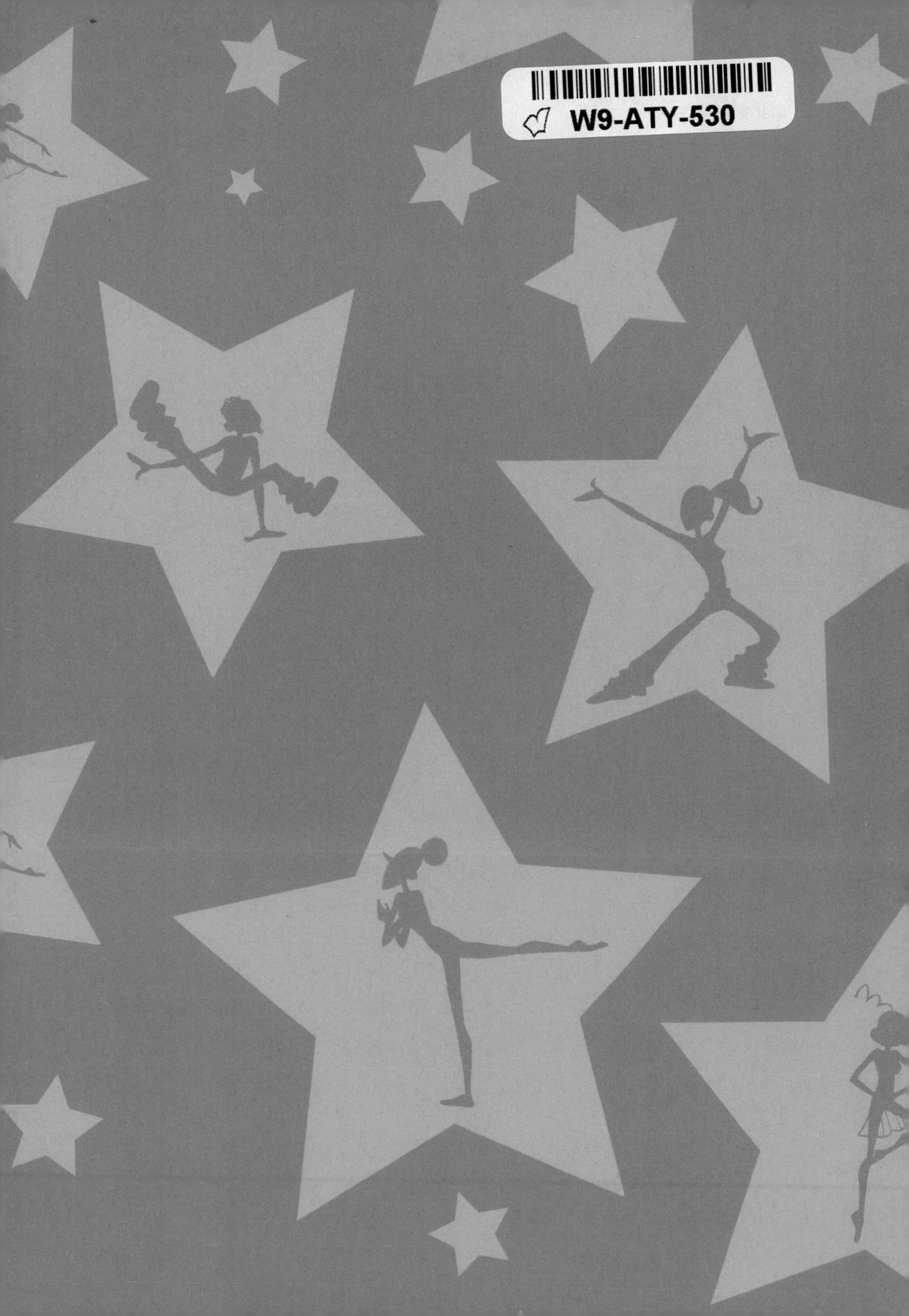

Dance Class

Crip • Art

Béka • Story

Maëla Cosson • Color

PAPERCUTZ™

New York

Dance Class Graphic Novels Available from PAPERCUTZ

Béka and Crip
Dance Class
So, You Think You Can Hip-Hop?
PAPERCUTZ

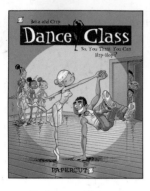

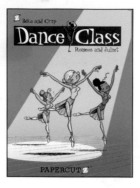

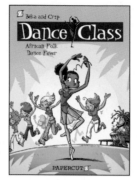

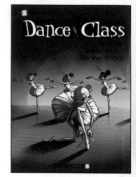

#1 "So, You Think You Can Hip-Hop?"

Béka and Crip
Dance Class
Romeos and Juliet
PAPERCUTZ

#2 "Romeos and Juliet"

Béka and Crip
Dance Class
African Folk Dance Fever
PAPERCUTZ

#3 "African Folk Dance Fever"

Dance Class

#4 "A Funny Thing Happened on the Way to Paris..."

Béka and Crip
Dance Class
To Russia, With Love
PAPERCUTZ

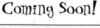

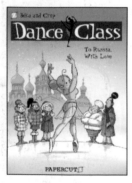

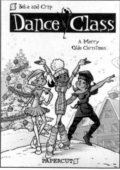

#5 "To Russia, With Love"

Coming Soon!

Béka and Crip
Dance Class
A Merry Olde Christmas
PAPERCUTZ

#6 "A Merry Olde Christmas"

DANCE CLASS graphic novels are available for $10.99 only in hardcover. Available from booksellers everywhere. You can also order online from Papercutz.com. Or call 1-800-886-1223, Monday through Friday, 9 - 5 EST. MC, Visa, and AmEx accepted. To order by mail, please add $4.00 for postage and handling for first book ordered, $1.00 for each additional book and make check payable to NBM Publishing. Send to: Papercutz, 160 Broadway, Suite 700, East Wing, New York, NY 10038.

DANCE CLASS graphic novels are also available digitally wherever e-books are sold.

Papercutz.com

Dance Class

DANCE CLASS #5
"To Russia, With Love"

Béka - writer
Crip - Artist
Maëla Cosson - Colorist
Joe Johnson - Translation
Tom Orzechowski - Lettering
Dawn K. Guzzo - Production
Beth Scorzato - Production Coordinator
Michael Petranek - Editor
Jim Salicrup
Editor-in-Chief

ISBN: 978-1-59707-423-0

Printed in China
July 2013 by New Era Printing LTD.
Unit C. 8/F Worldwide Centre
123 Chung Tau, Kowloon, Hong Kong

Papercutz books may be purchased for business or promotional use. For information on bulk purchases please contact Macmillan Corporate and Premium Sales Department at (800) 221-7945 x5442.

Distributed by Macmillan
First Papercutz Printing

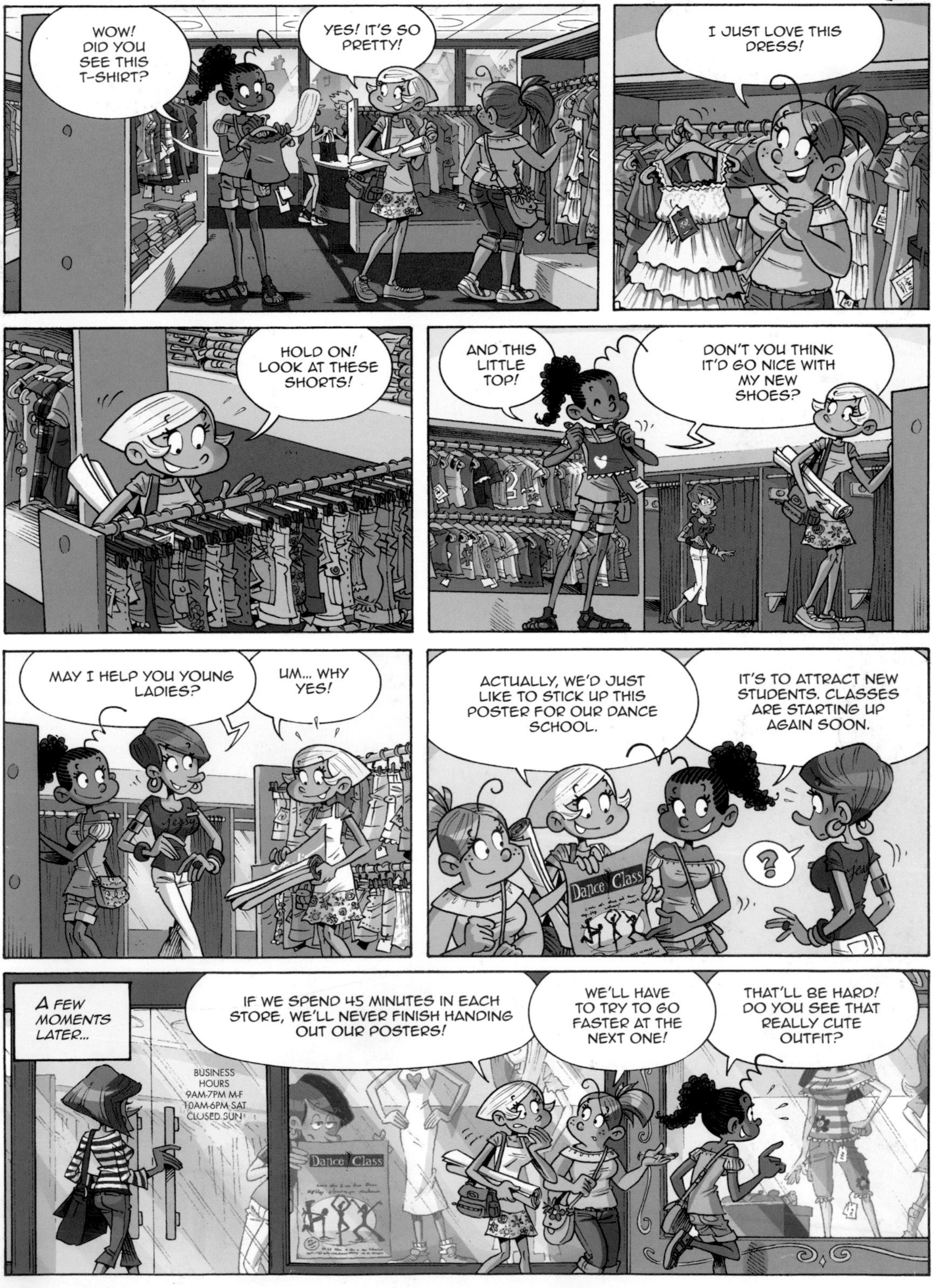
WOW! DID YOU SEE THIS T-SHIRT?
YES! IT'S SO PRETTY!
I JUST LOVE THIS DRESS!
HOLD ON! LOOK AT THESE SHORTS!
AND THIS LITTLE TOP!
DON'T YOU THINK IT'D GO NICE WITH MY NEW SHOES?
MAY I HELP YOU YOUNG LADIES?
UM... WHY YES!
ACTUALLY, WE'D JUST LIKE TO STICK UP THIS POSTER FOR OUR DANCE SCHOOL.
IT'S TO ATTRACT NEW STUDENTS. CLASSES ARE STARTING UP AGAIN SOON.
Dance Class
?
A FEW MOMENTS LATER...
IF WE SPEND 45 MINUTES IN EACH STORE, WE'LL NEVER FINISH HANDING OUT OUR POSTERS!
WE'LL HAVE TO TRY TO GO FASTER AT THE NEXT ONE!
THAT'LL BE HARD! DO YOU SEE THAT REALLY CUTE OUTFIT?
BUSINESS HOURS 9AM-7PM M-F 10AM-6PM SAT CLOSED SUN
Dance Class

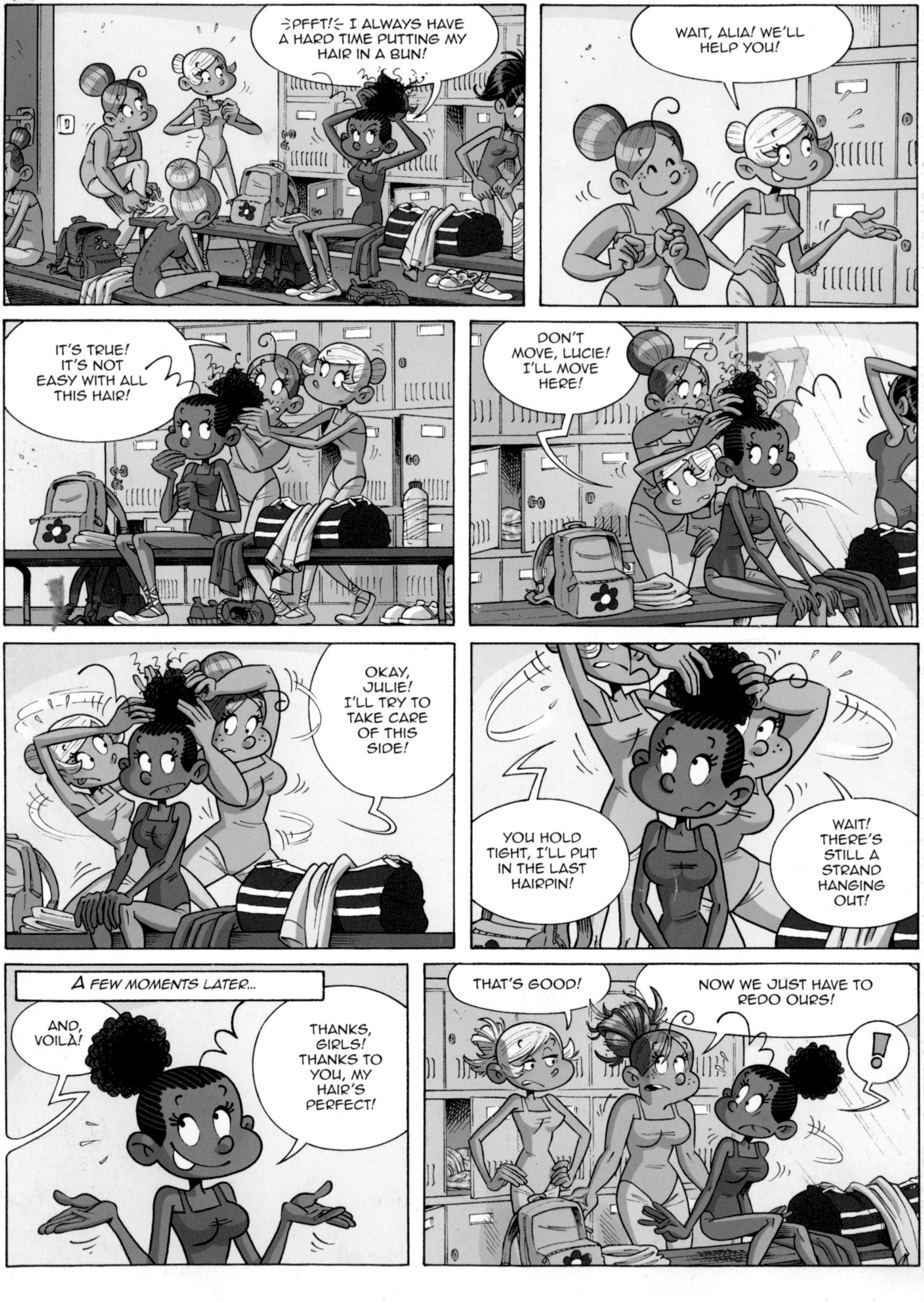

⋛PFFT!⋚ I ALWAYS HAVE A HARD TIME PUTTING MY HAIR IN A BUN!
WAIT, ALIA! WE'LL HELP YOU!
IT'S TRUE! IT'S NOT EASY WITH ALL THIS HAIR!
DON'T MOVE, LUCIE! I'LL MOVE HERE!
OKAY, JULIE! I'LL TRY TO TAKE CARE OF THIS SIDE!
YOU HOLD TIGHT, I'LL PUT IN THE LAST HAIRPIN!
WAIT! THERE'S STILL A STRAND HANGING OUT!
A FEW MOMENTS LATER...
AND, VOILÀ!
THANKS, GIRLS! THANKS TO YOU, MY HAIR'S PERFECT!
THAT'S GOOD!
NOW WE JUST HAVE TO REDO OURS!
!

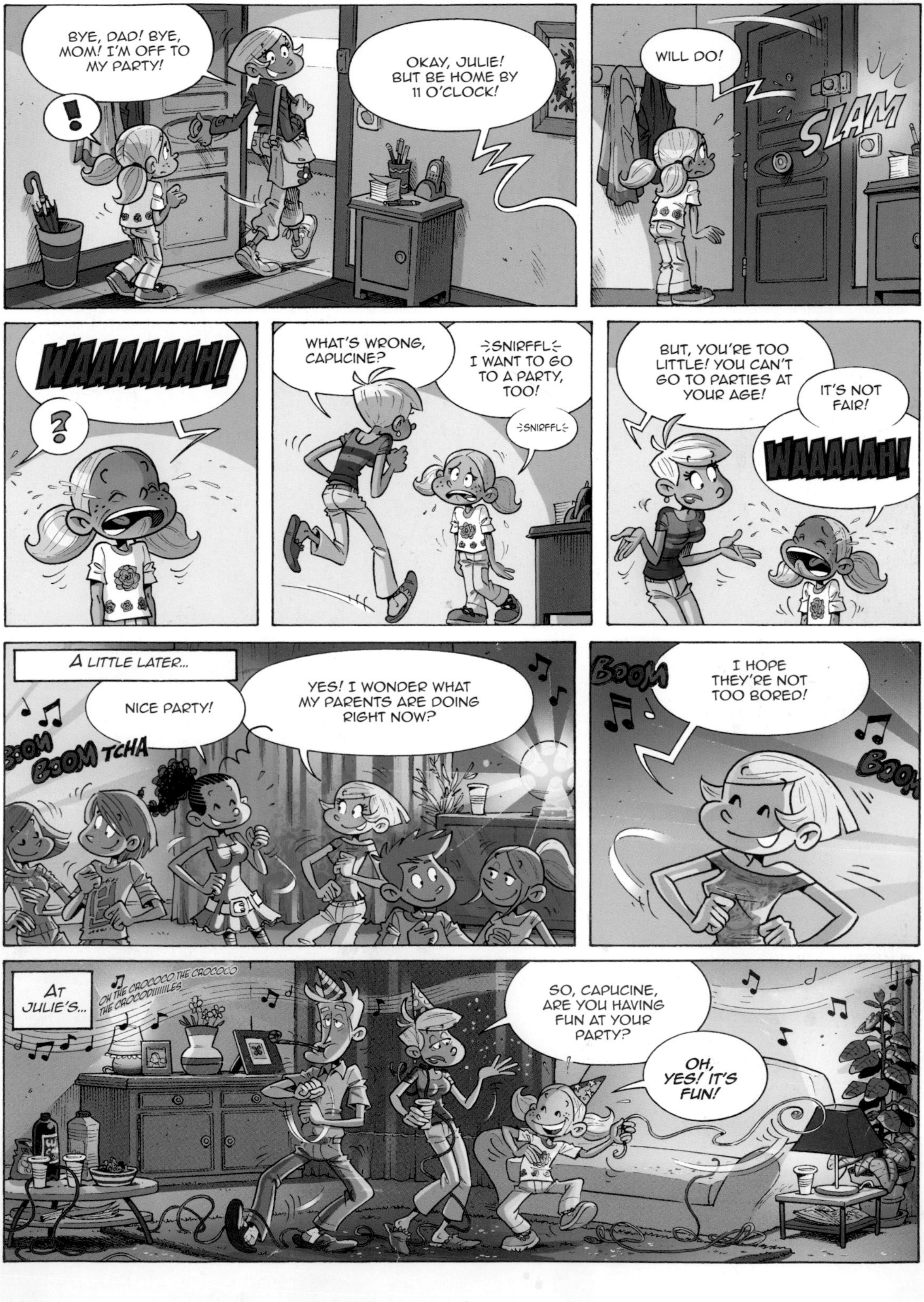
BYE, DAD! BYE, MOM! I'M OFF TO MY PARTY!
!
OKAY, JULIE! BUT BE HOME BY 11 O'CLOCK!
WILL DO!
SLAM
WAAAAAAH!
?
WHAT'S WRONG, CAPUCINE?
SNIRFFL I WANT TO GO TO A PARTY, TOO!
SNIRFFL
BUT, YOU'RE TOO LITTLE! YOU CAN'T GO TO PARTIES AT YOUR AGE!
IT'S NOT FAIR!
WAAAAAH!
A LITTLE LATER...
NICE PARTY!
YES! I WONDER WHAT MY PARENTS ARE DOING RIGHT NOW?
BOOM BOOM TCHA
BOOM
I HOPE THEY'RE NOT TOO BORED!
BOOM
AT JULIE'S...
OH THE CROCOCO THE CROCOCO THE CROCODIIIIIILES
SO, CAPUCINE, ARE YOU HAVING FUN AT YOUR PARTY?
!
OH, YES! IT'S FUN!

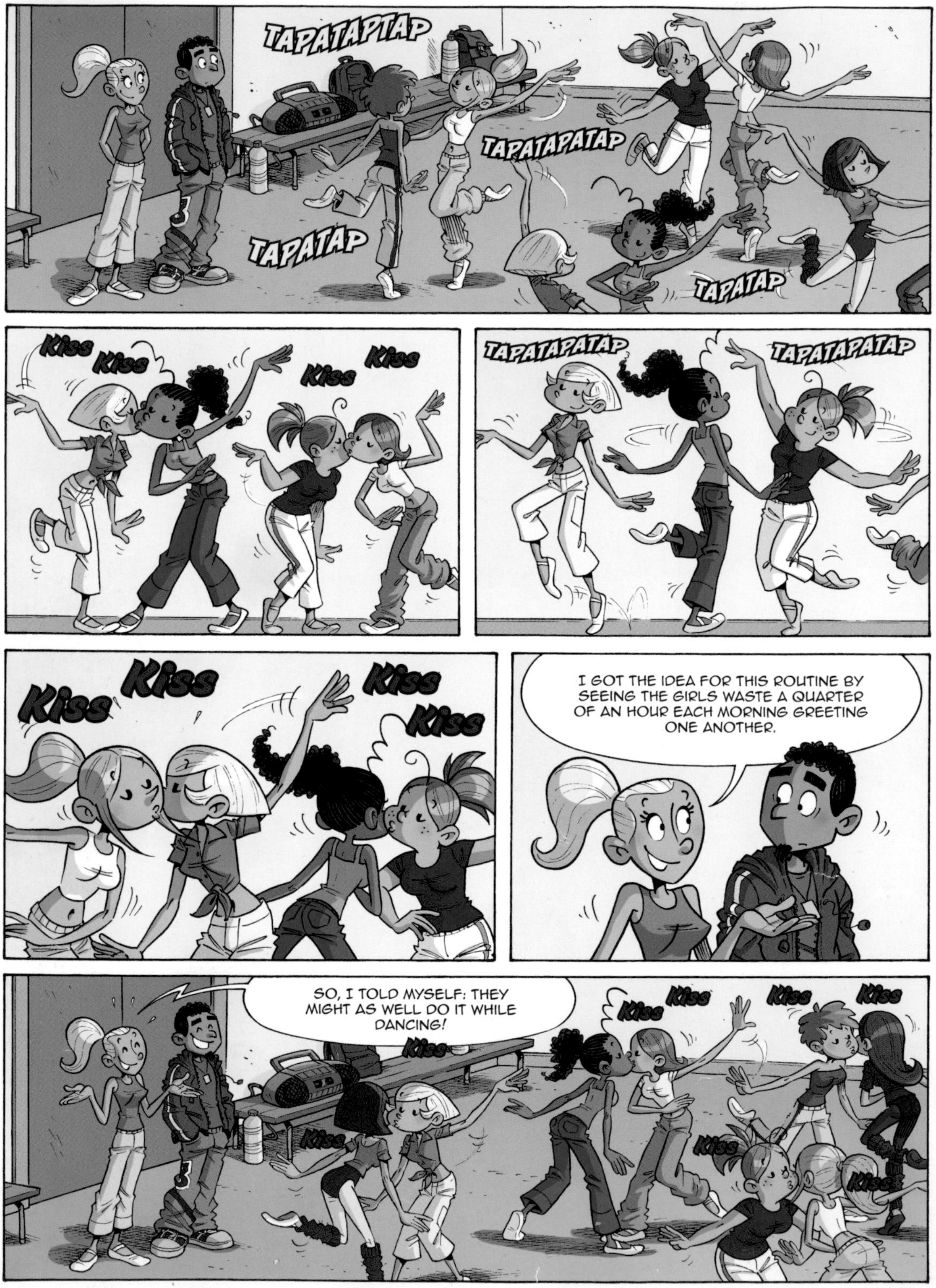
TAPATAPTAP
TAPATAPATAP
TAPATAP
TAPATAP
Kiss
Kiss
Kiss
Kiss
TAPATAPATAP
TAPATAPATAP
Kiss
Kiss
Kiss
Kiss
I GOT THE IDEA FOR THIS ROUTINE BY SEEING THE GIRLS WASTE A QUARTER OF AN HOUR EACH MORNING GREETING ONE ANOTHER.
SO, I TOLD MYSELF: THEY MIGHT AS WELL DO IT WHILE DANCING!
Kiss
Kiss
Kiss
Kiss
Kiss
Kiss
Kiss

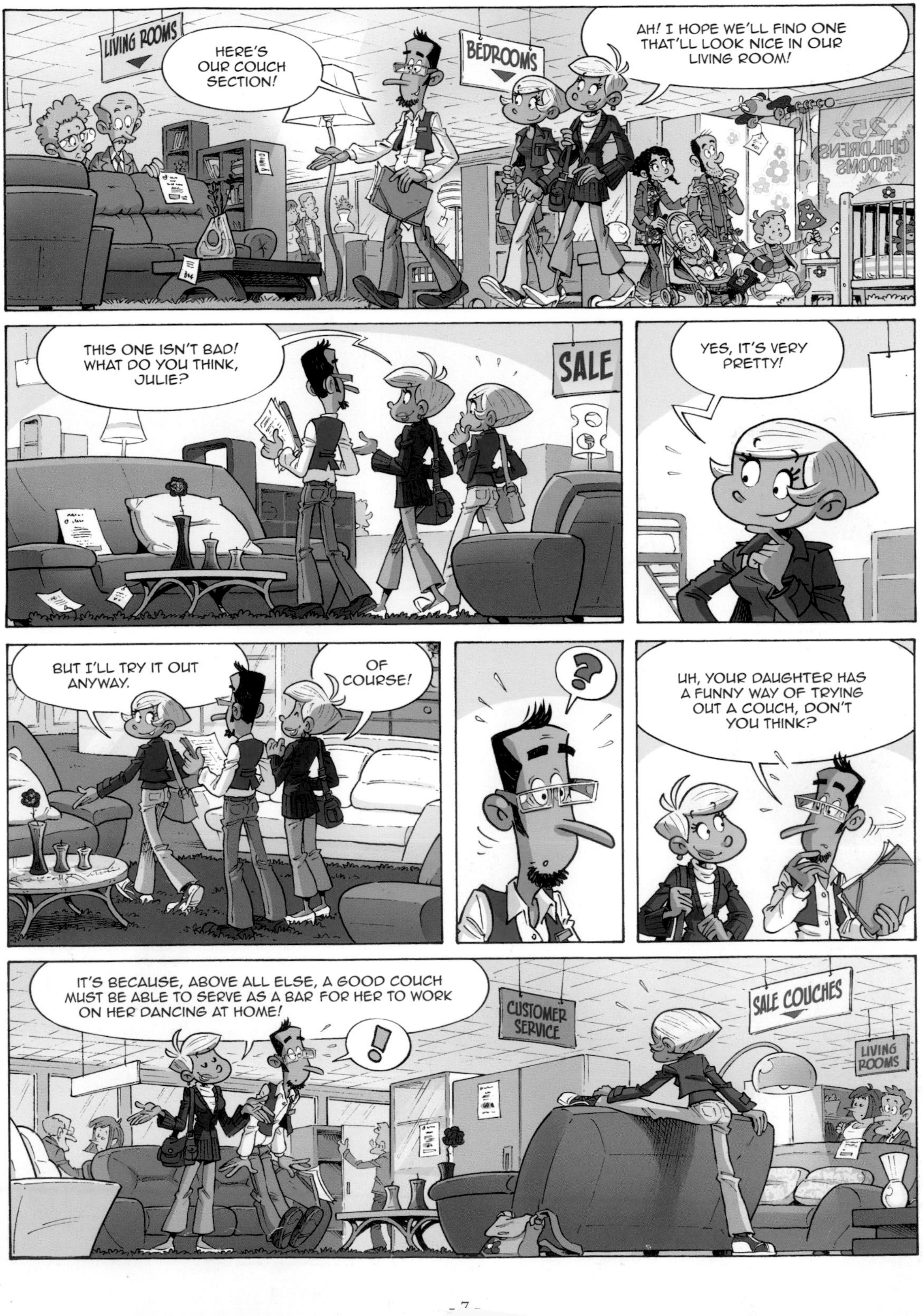
LIVING ROOMS
HERE'S OUR COUCH SECTION!
BEDROOMS
AH! I HOPE WE'LL FIND ONE THAT'LL LOOK NICE IN OUR LIVING ROOM!
-25% CHILDRENS ROOMS
THIS ONE ISN'T BAD! WHAT DO YOU THINK, JULIE?
SALE
YES, IT'S VERY PRETTY!
BUT I'LL TRY IT OUT ANYWAY.
OF COURSE!
?
UH, YOUR DAUGHTER HAS A FUNNY WAY OF TRYING OUT A COUCH, DON'T YOU THINK?
IT'S BECAUSE, ABOVE ALL ELSE, A GOOD COUCH MUST BE ABLE TO SERVE AS A BAR FOR HER TO WORK ON HER DANCING AT HOME!
!
CUSTOMER SERVICE
SALE COUCHES
LIVING ROOMS

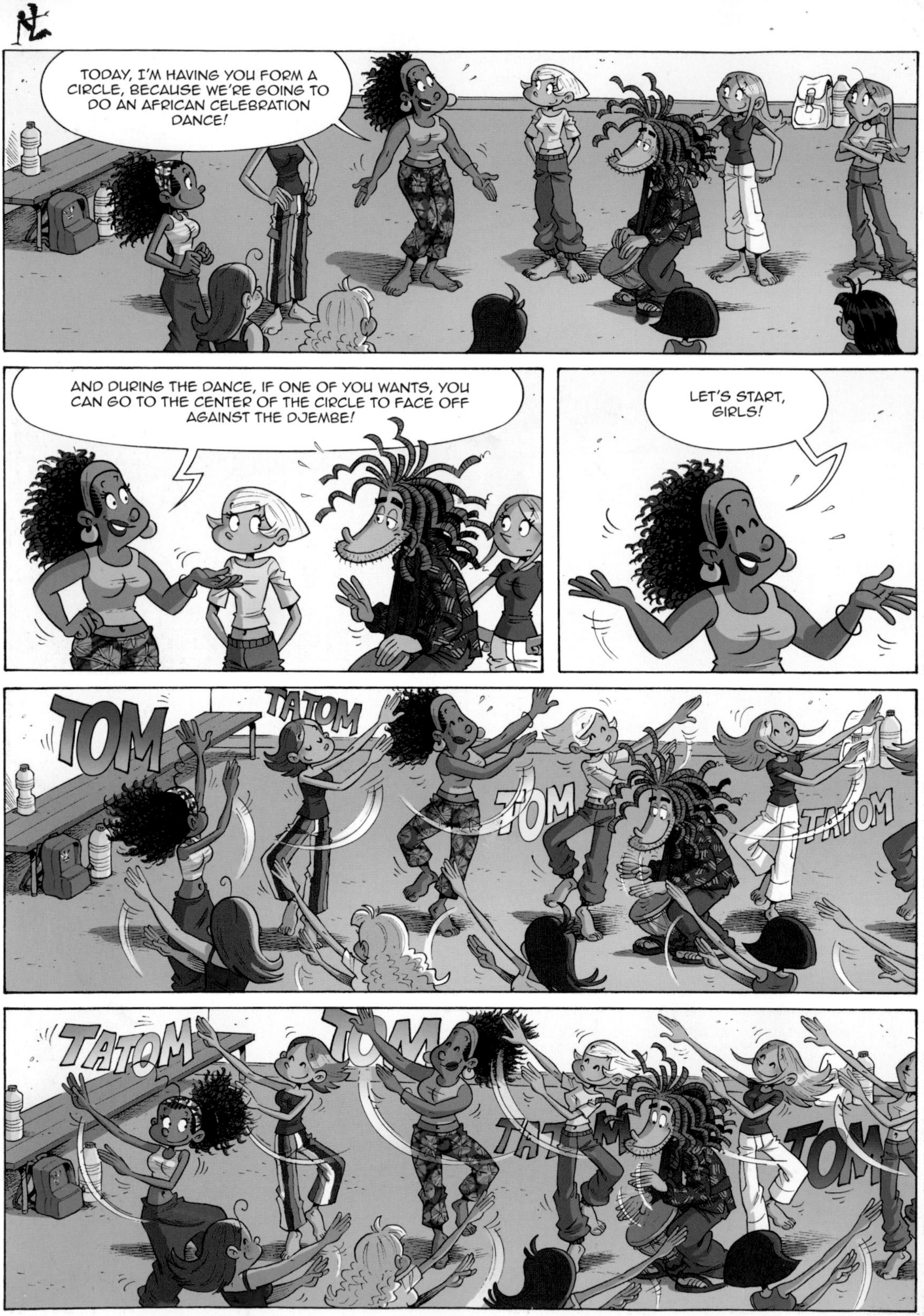

TODAY, I'M HAVING YOU FORM A CIRCLE, BECAUSE WE'RE GOING TO DO AN AFRICAN CELEBRATION DANCE!
AND DURING THE DANCE, IF ONE OF YOU WANTS, YOU CAN GO TO THE CENTER OF THE CIRCLE TO FACE OFF AGAINST THE DJEMBE!
LET'S START, GIRLS!
TOM
TATOM
TOM
TATOM
TATOM
TOM
TATOM
TOM

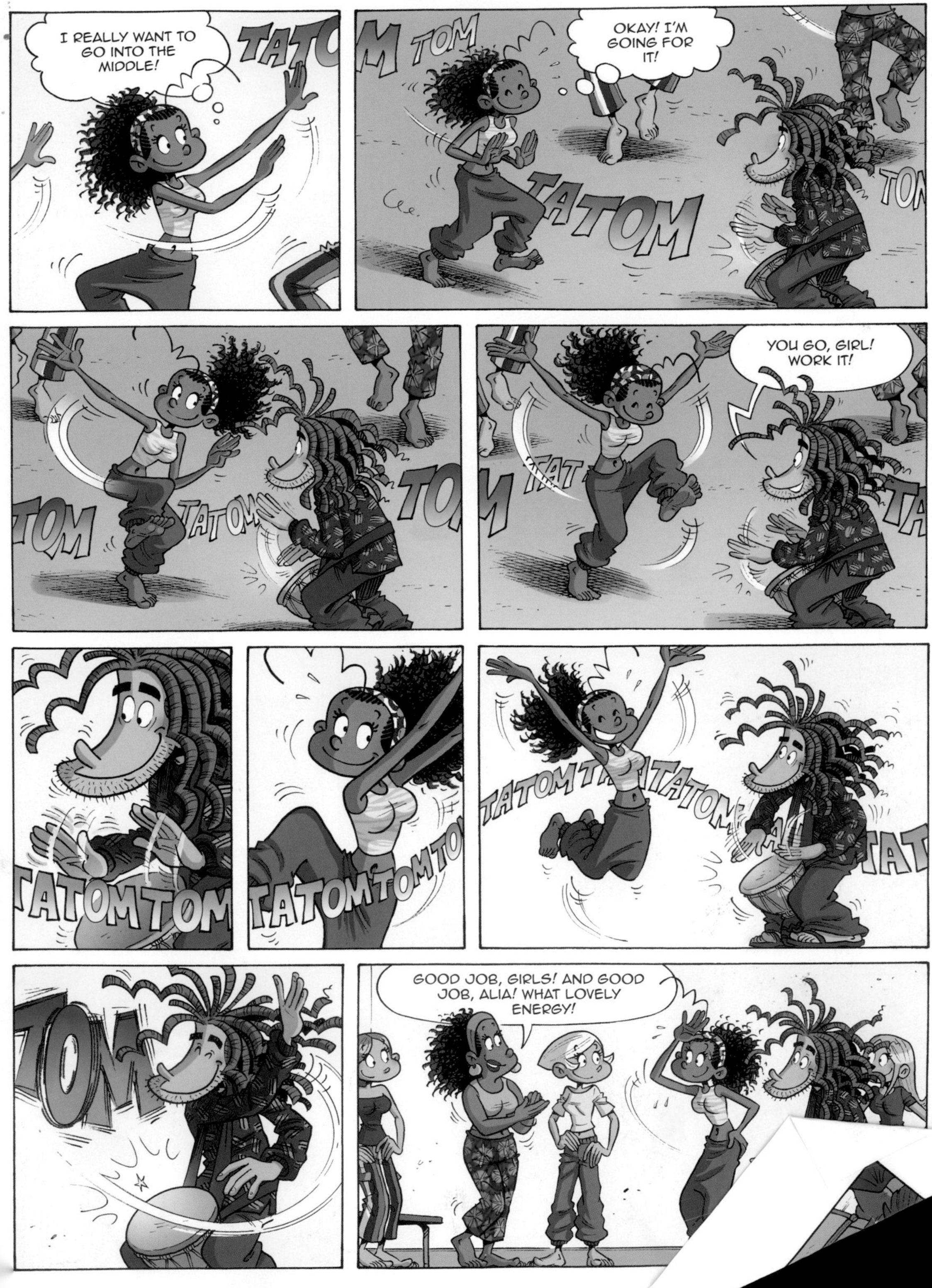
I REALLY WANT TO GO INTO THE MIDDLE!
TATOM TOM
OKAY! I'M GOING FOR IT!
TATOM
TOM
TATOM
TATOM
TOM
YOU GO, GIRL! WORK IT!
TATOMTOM
TATOMTOMTOM
TATOM
TATOM
TAT
TOM
GOOD JOB, GIRLS! AND GOOD JOB, ALIA! WHAT LOVELY ENERGY!

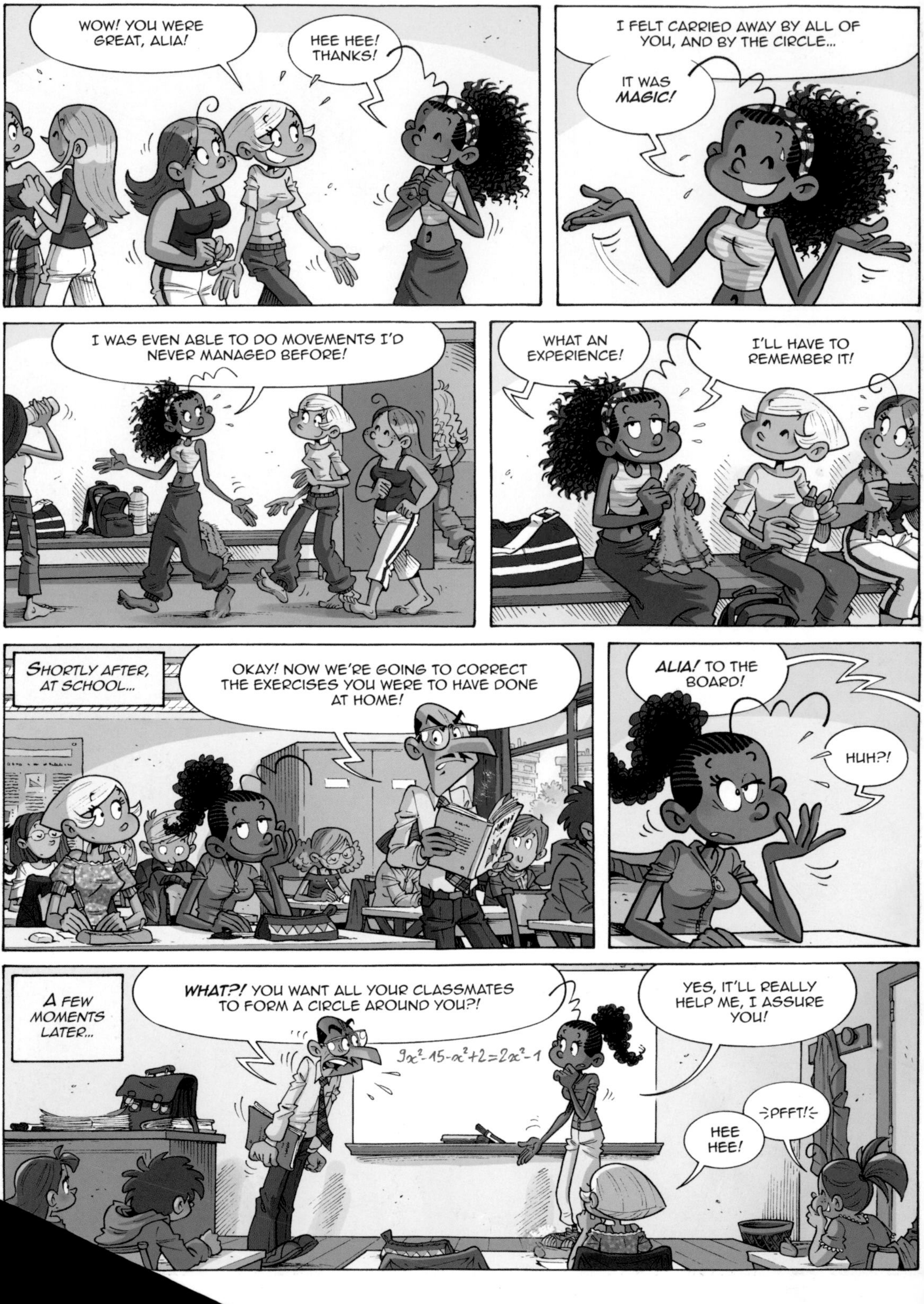
WOW! YOU WERE GREAT, ALIA!
HEE HEE! THANKS!
I FELT CARRIED AWAY BY ALL OF YOU, AND BY THE CIRCLE...
IT WAS *MAGIC!*
I WAS EVEN ABLE TO DO MOVEMENTS I'D NEVER MANAGED BEFORE!
WHAT AN EXPERIENCE!
I'LL HAVE TO REMEMBER IT!
SHORTLY AFTER, AT SCHOOL...
OKAY! NOW WE'RE GOING TO CORRECT THE EXERCISES YOU WERE TO HAVE DONE AT HOME!
ALIA! TO THE BOARD!
HUH?!
A FEW MOMENTS LATER...
WHAT?! YOU WANT ALL YOUR CLASSMATES TO FORM A CIRCLE AROUND YOU?!
$9x^2-15-x^2+2=2x^2-1$
YES, IT'LL REALLY HELP ME, I ASSURE YOU!
PFFT!
HEE HEE!

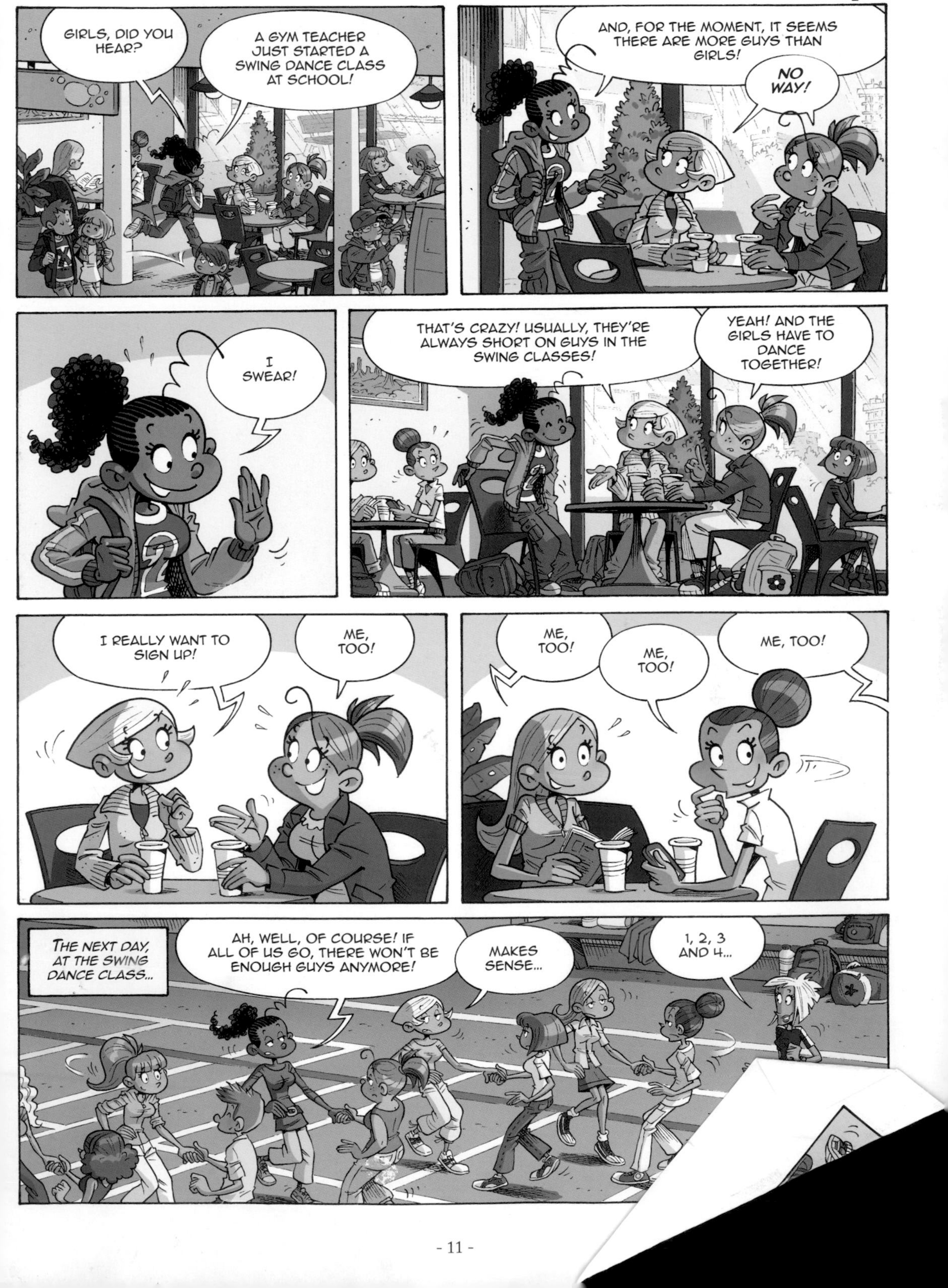

GIRLS, DID YOU HEAR?
A GYM TEACHER JUST STARTED A SWING DANCE CLASS AT SCHOOL!
AND, FOR THE MOMENT, IT SEEMS THERE ARE MORE GUYS THAN GIRLS!
NO WAY!
I SWEAR!
THAT'S CRAZY! USUALLY, THEY'RE ALWAYS SHORT ON GUYS IN THE SWING CLASSES!
YEAH! AND THE GIRLS HAVE TO DANCE TOGETHER!
I REALLY WANT TO SIGN UP!
ME, TOO!
ME, TOO!
ME, TOO!
ME, TOO!
THE NEXT DAY, AT THE SWING DANCE CLASS...
AH, WELL, OF COURSE! IF ALL OF US GO, THERE WON'T BE ENOUGH GUYS ANYMORE!
MAKES SENSE...
1, 2, 3 AND 4...

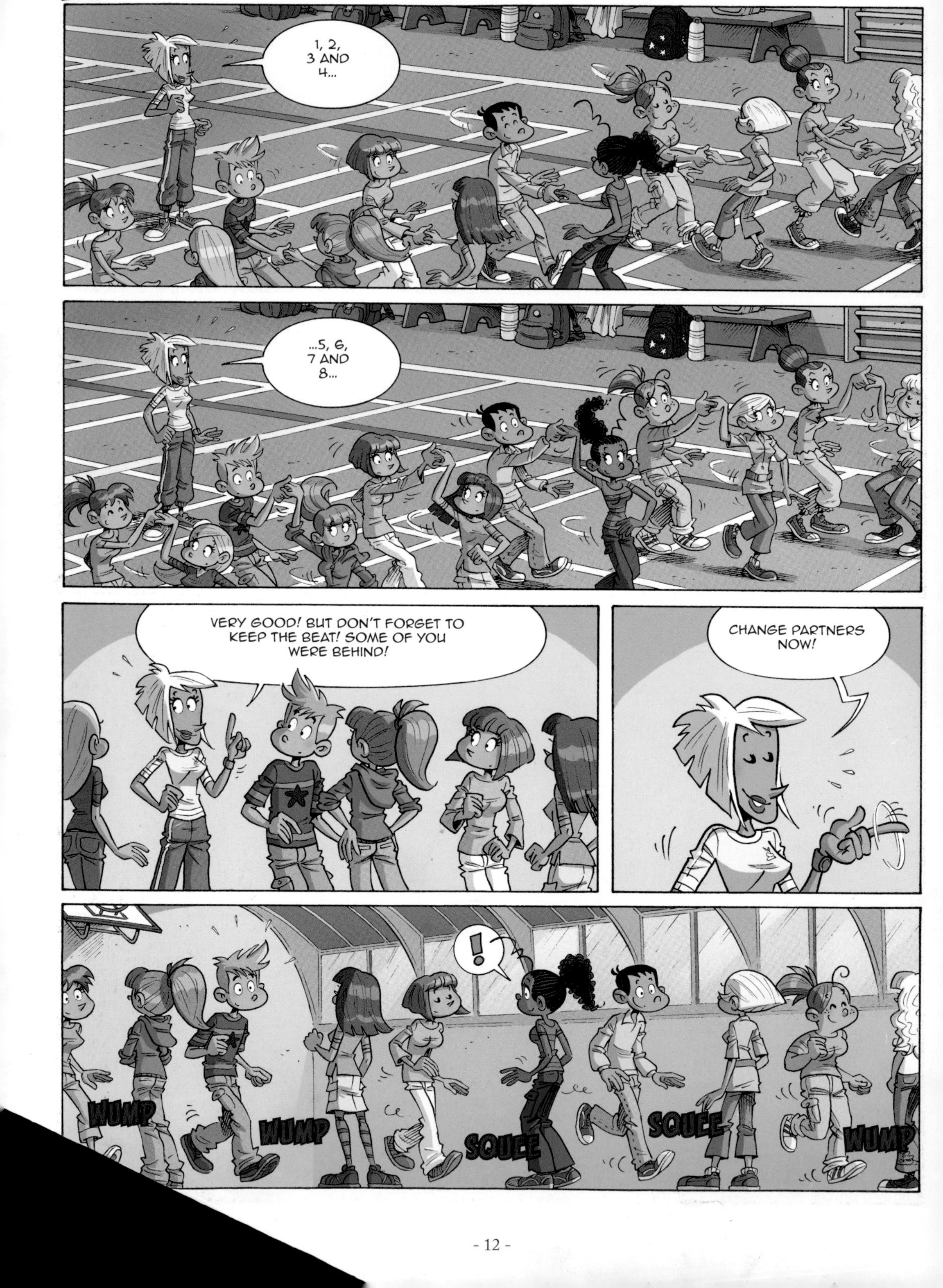
1, 2, 3 AND 4...
...5, 6, 7 AND 8...
VERY GOOD! BUT DON'T FORGET TO KEEP THE BEAT! SOME OF YOU WERE BEHIND!
CHANGE PARTNERS NOW!
!
WUMP
WUMP
SQUEE
SQUEE
WUMP

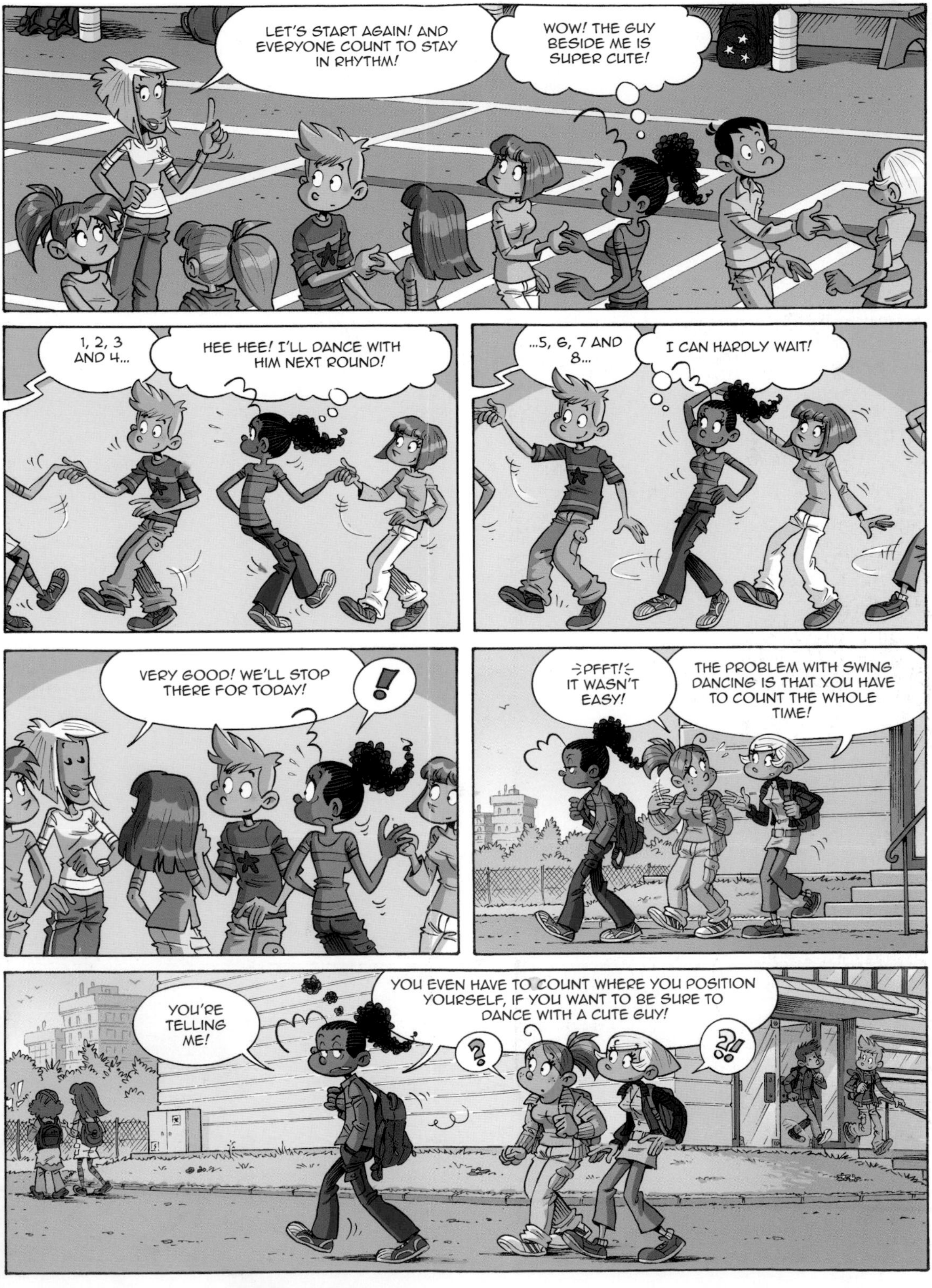
LET'S START AGAIN! AND EVERYONE COUNT TO STAY IN RHYTHM!
WOW! THE GUY BESIDE ME IS SUPER CUTE!
1, 2, 3 AND 4...
HEE HEE! I'LL DANCE WITH HIM NEXT ROUND!
...5, 6, 7 AND 8...
I CAN HARDLY WAIT!
VERY GOOD! WE'LL STOP THERE FOR TODAY!
!
PFFT! IT WASN'T EASY!
THE PROBLEM WITH SWING DANCING IS THAT YOU HAVE TO COUNT THE WHOLE TIME!
YOU'RE TELLING ME!
YOU EVEN HAVE TO COUNT WHERE YOU POSITION YOURSELF, IF YOU WANT TO BE SURE TO DANCE WITH A CUTE GUY!
?
?!!

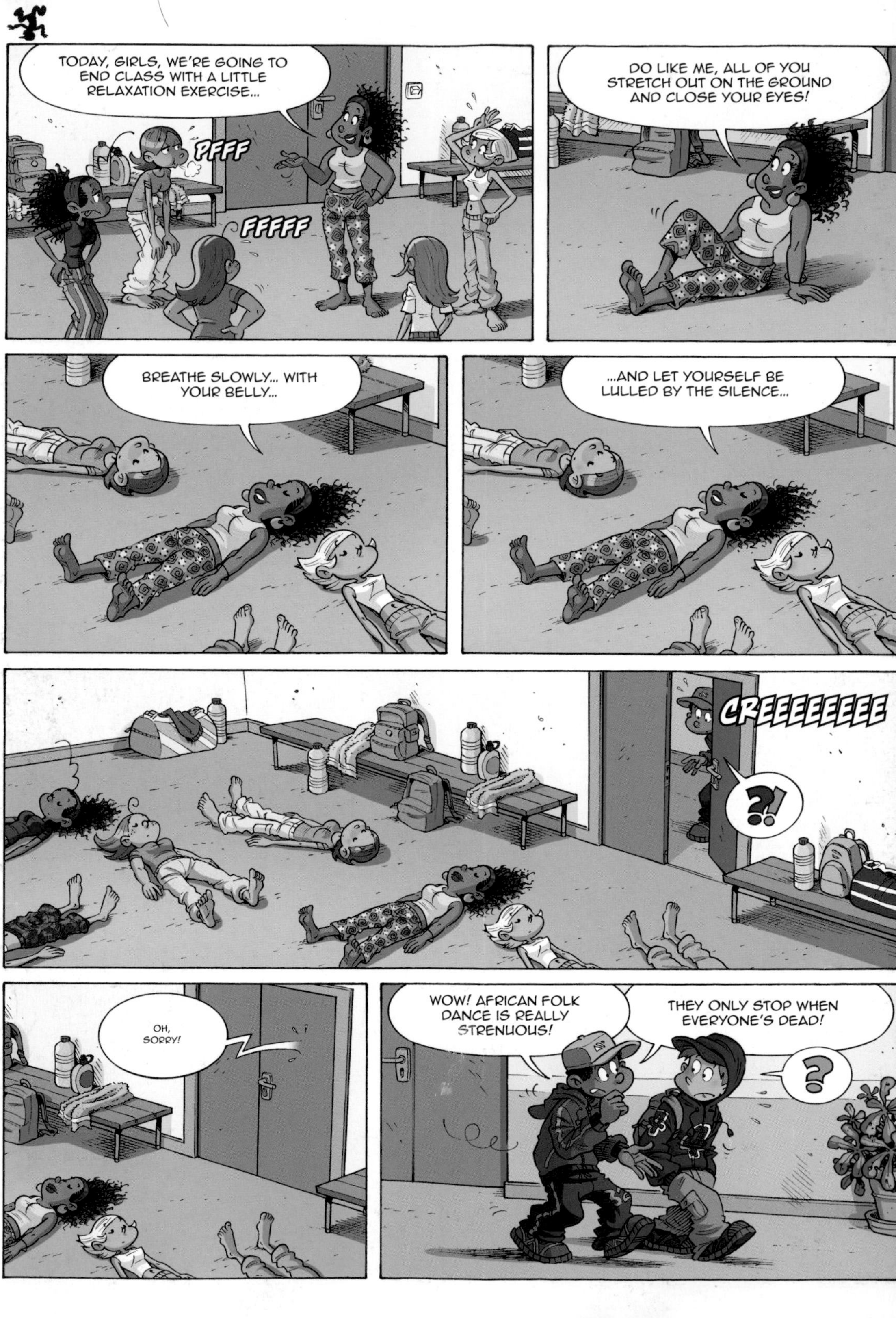
TODAY, GIRLS, WE'RE GOING TO END CLASS WITH A LITTLE RELAXATION EXERCISE...
PFFF
FFFFF
DO LIKE ME, ALL OF YOU STRETCH OUT ON THE GROUND AND CLOSE YOUR EYES!
BREATHE SLOWLY... WITH YOUR BELLY...
...AND LET YOURSELF BE LULLED BY THE SILENCE...
CREEEEEEEE
?!
OH, SORRY!
WOW! AFRICAN FOLK DANCE IS REALLY STRENUOUS!
THEY ONLY STOP WHEN EVERYONE'S DEAD!
?

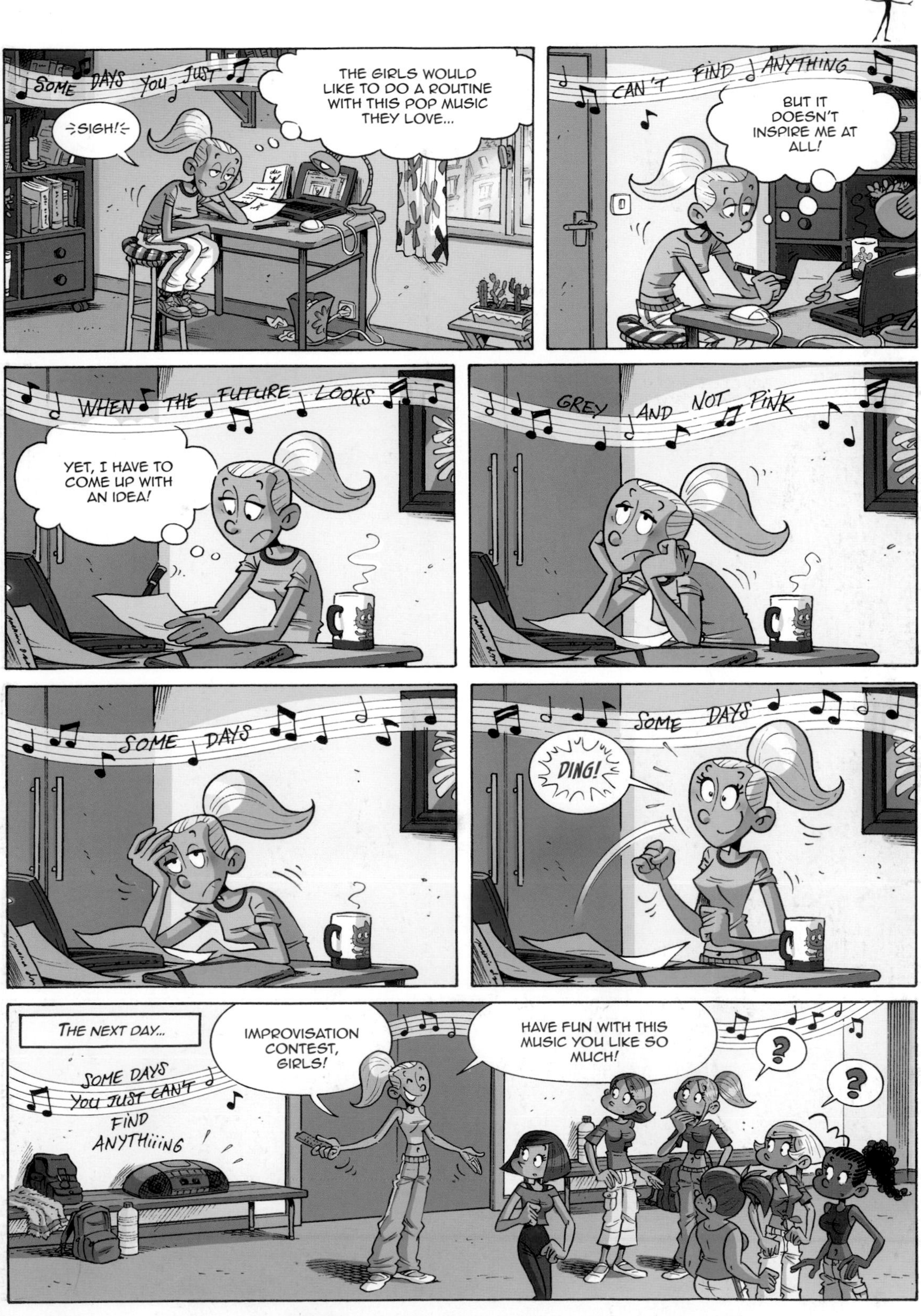
SOME DAYS YOU JUST
SIGH!
THE GIRLS WOULD LIKE TO DO A ROUTINE WITH THIS POP MUSIC THEY LOVE...
CAN'T FIND ANYTHING
BUT IT DOESN'T INSPIRE ME AT ALL!
WHEN THE FUTURE LOOKS
YET, I HAVE TO COME UP WITH AN IDEA!
GREY AND NOT PINK
SOME DAYS
SOME DAYS
DING!
THE NEXT DAY...
SOME DAYS YOU JUST CAN'T FIND ANYTHiiiNG
IMPROVISATION CONTEST, GIRLS!
HAVE FUN WITH THIS MUSIC YOU LIKE SO MUCH!
?
?

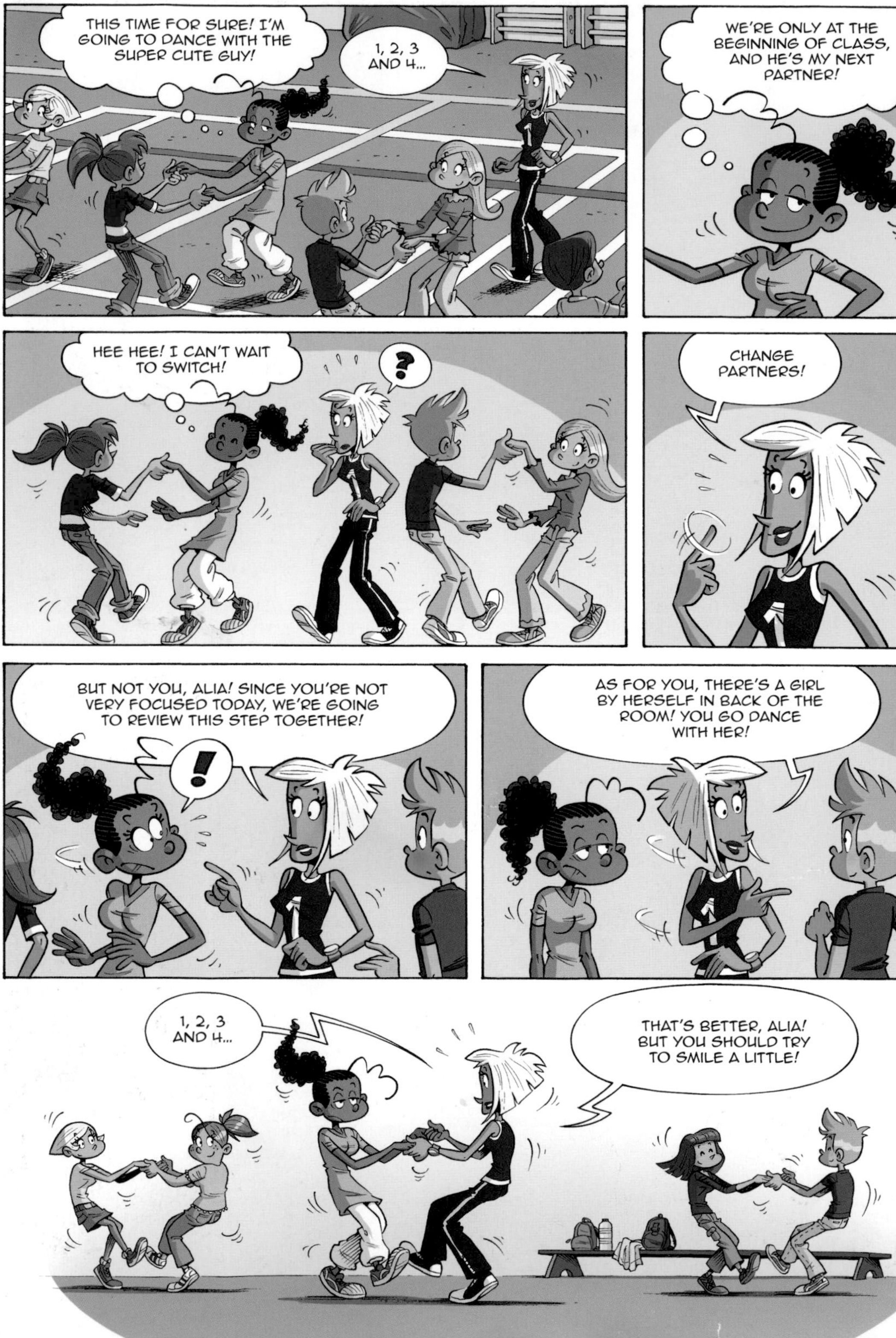

THIS TIME FOR SURE! I'M GOING TO DANCE WITH THE SUPER CUTE GUY!
1, 2, 3 AND 4...
WE'RE ONLY AT THE BEGINNING OF CLASS, AND HE'S MY NEXT PARTNER!
HEE HEE! I CAN'T WAIT TO SWITCH!
?
CHANGE PARTNERS!
BUT NOT YOU, ALIA! SINCE YOU'RE NOT VERY FOCUSED TODAY, WE'RE GOING TO REVIEW THIS STEP TOGETHER!
!
AS FOR YOU, THERE'S A GIRL BY HERSELF IN BACK OF THE ROOM! YOU GO DANCE WITH HER!
1, 2, 3 AND 4...
THAT'S BETTER, ALIA! BUT YOU SHOULD TRY TO SMILE A LITTLE!

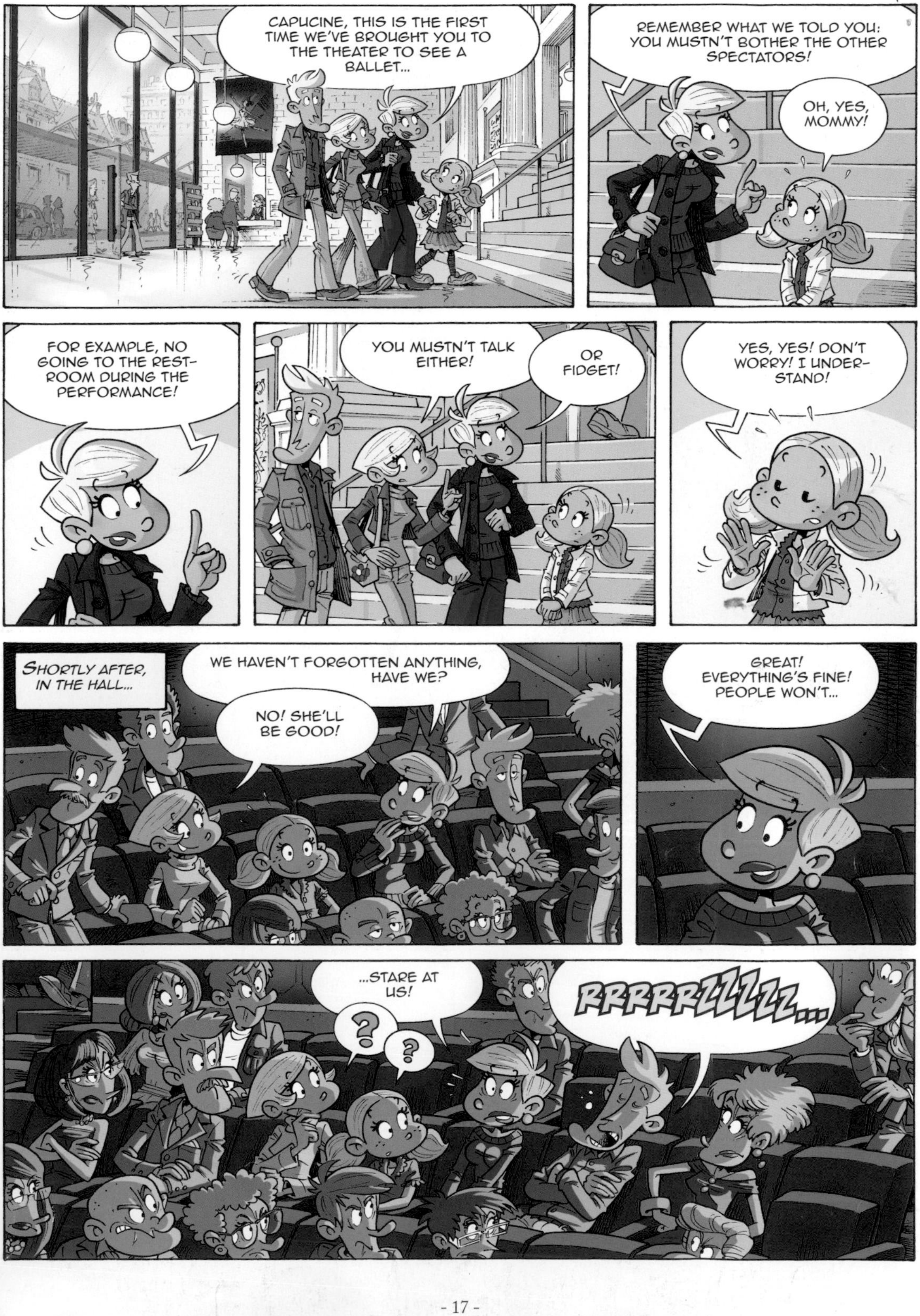
CAPUCINE, THIS IS THE FIRST TIME WE'VE BROUGHT YOU TO THE THEATER TO SEE A BALLET...
REMEMBER WHAT WE TOLD YOU: YOU MUSTN'T BOTHER THE OTHER SPECTATORS!
OH, YES, MOMMY!
FOR EXAMPLE, NO GOING TO THE REST-ROOM DURING THE PERFORMANCE!
YOU MUSTN'T TALK EITHER!
OR FIDGET!
YES, YES! DON'T WORRY! I UNDER-STAND!
SHORTLY AFTER, IN THE HALL...
WE HAVEN'T FORGOTTEN ANYTHING, HAVE WE?
NO! SHE'LL BE GOOD!
GREAT! EVERYTHING'S FINE! PEOPLE WON'T...
...STARE AT US!
?
?
RRRRRZZZZZ...

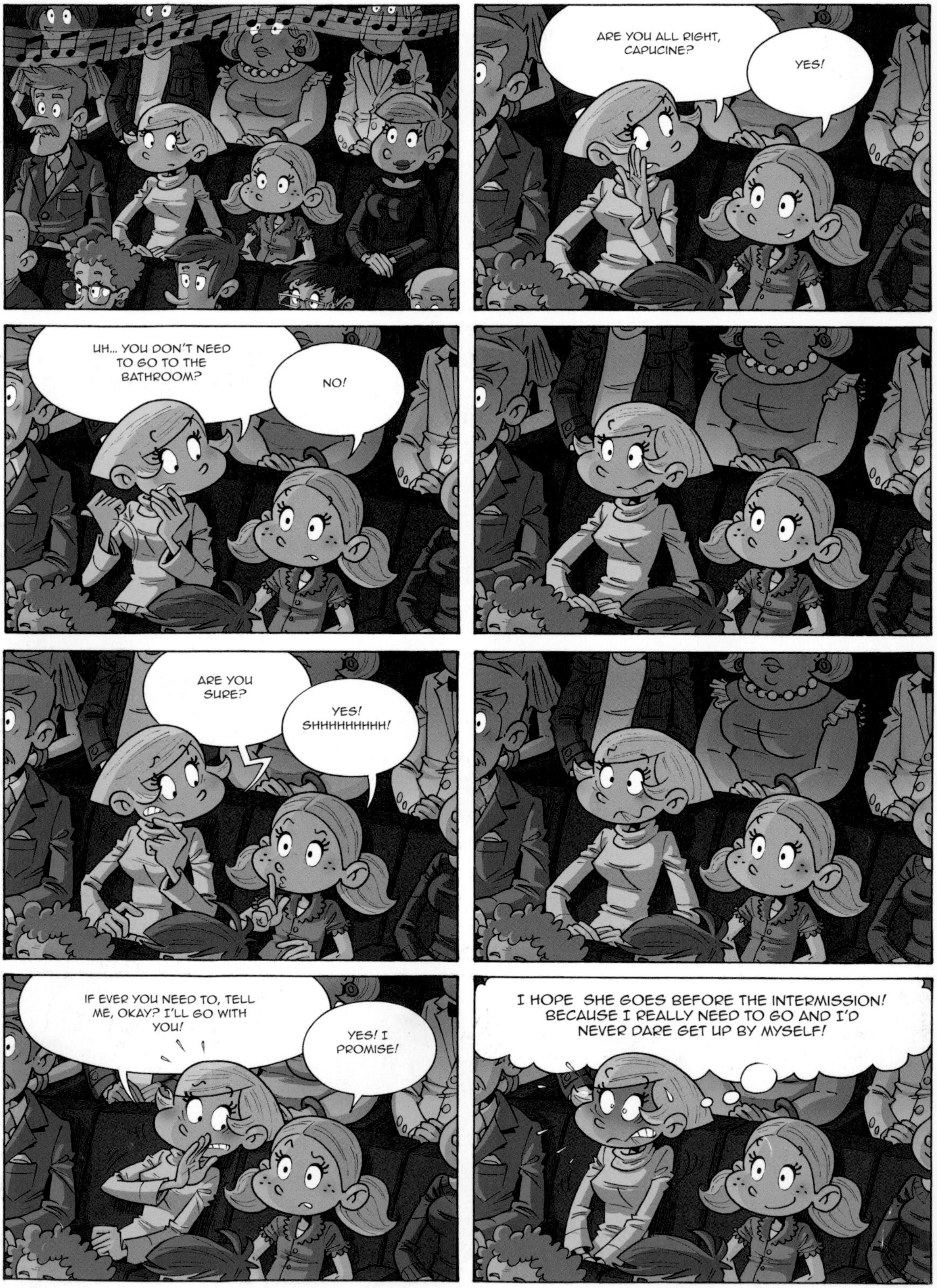

ARE YOU ALL RIGHT, CAPUCINE?
YES!
UH... YOU DON'T NEED TO GO TO THE BATHROOM?
NO!
ARE YOU SURE?
YES! SHHHHHHHHH!
IF EVER YOU NEED TO, TELL ME, OKAY? I'LL GO WITH YOU!
YES! I PROMISE!
I HOPE SHE GOES BEFORE THE INTERMISSION! BECAUSE I REALLY NEED TO GO AND I'D NEVER DARE GET UP BY MYSELF!

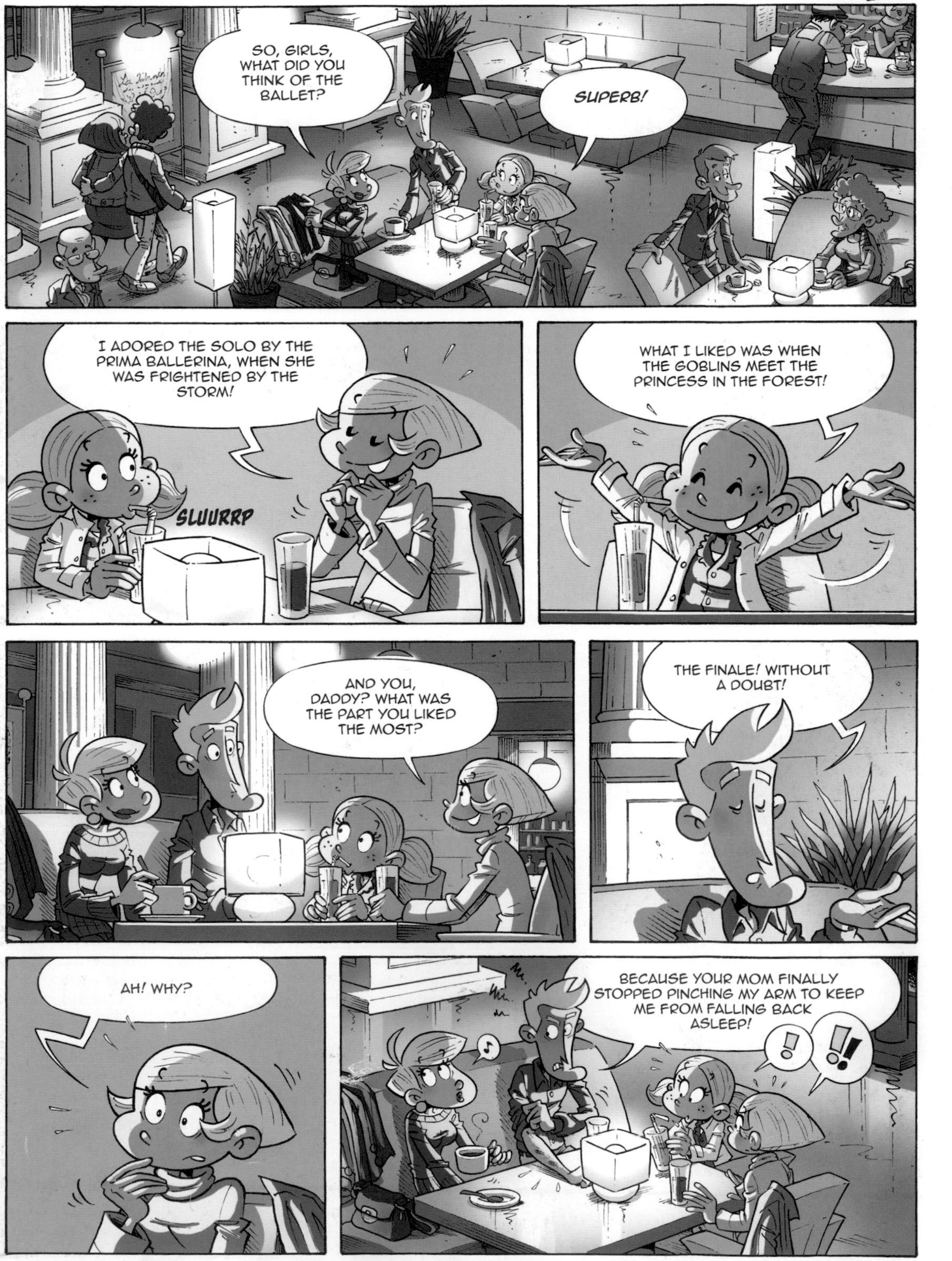
SO, GIRLS, WHAT DID YOU THINK OF THE BALLET?
SUPERB!
I ADORED THE SOLO BY THE PRIMA BALLERINA, WHEN SHE WAS FRIGHTENED BY THE STORM!
SLUURRP
WHAT I LIKED WAS WHEN THE GOBLINS MEET THE PRINCESS IN THE FOREST!
AND YOU, DADDY? WHAT WAS THE PART YOU LIKED THE MOST?
THE FINALE! WITHOUT A DOUBT!
AH! WHY?
BECAUSE YOUR MOM FINALLY STOPPED PINCHING MY ARM TO KEEP ME FROM FALLING BACK ASLEEP!
!
!!

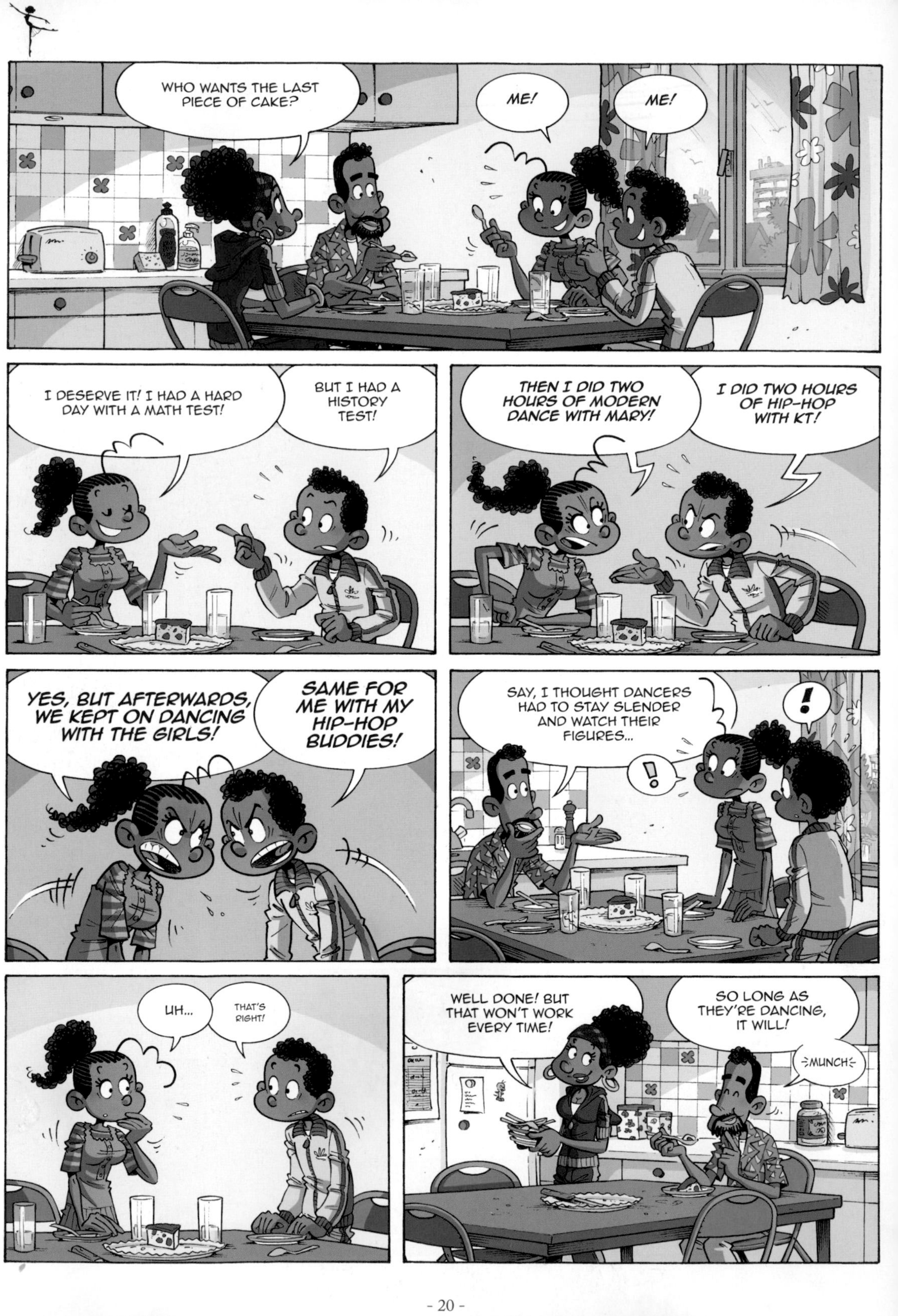
WHO WANTS THE LAST PIECE OF CAKE?
ME!
ME!
I DESERVE IT! I HAD A HARD DAY WITH A MATH TEST!
BUT I HAD A HISTORY TEST!
THEN I DID TWO HOURS OF MODERN DANCE WITH MARY!
I DID TWO HOURS OF HIP-HOP WITH KT!
YES, BUT AFTERWARDS, WE KEPT ON DANCING WITH THE GIRLS!
SAME FOR ME WITH MY HIP-HOP BUDDIES!
SAY, I THOUGHT DANCERS HAD TO STAY SLENDER AND WATCH THEIR FIGURES...
!
!
UH...
THAT'S RIGHT!
WELL DONE! BUT THAT WON'T WORK EVERY TIME!
SO LONG AS THEY'RE DANCING, IT WILL!
MUNCH

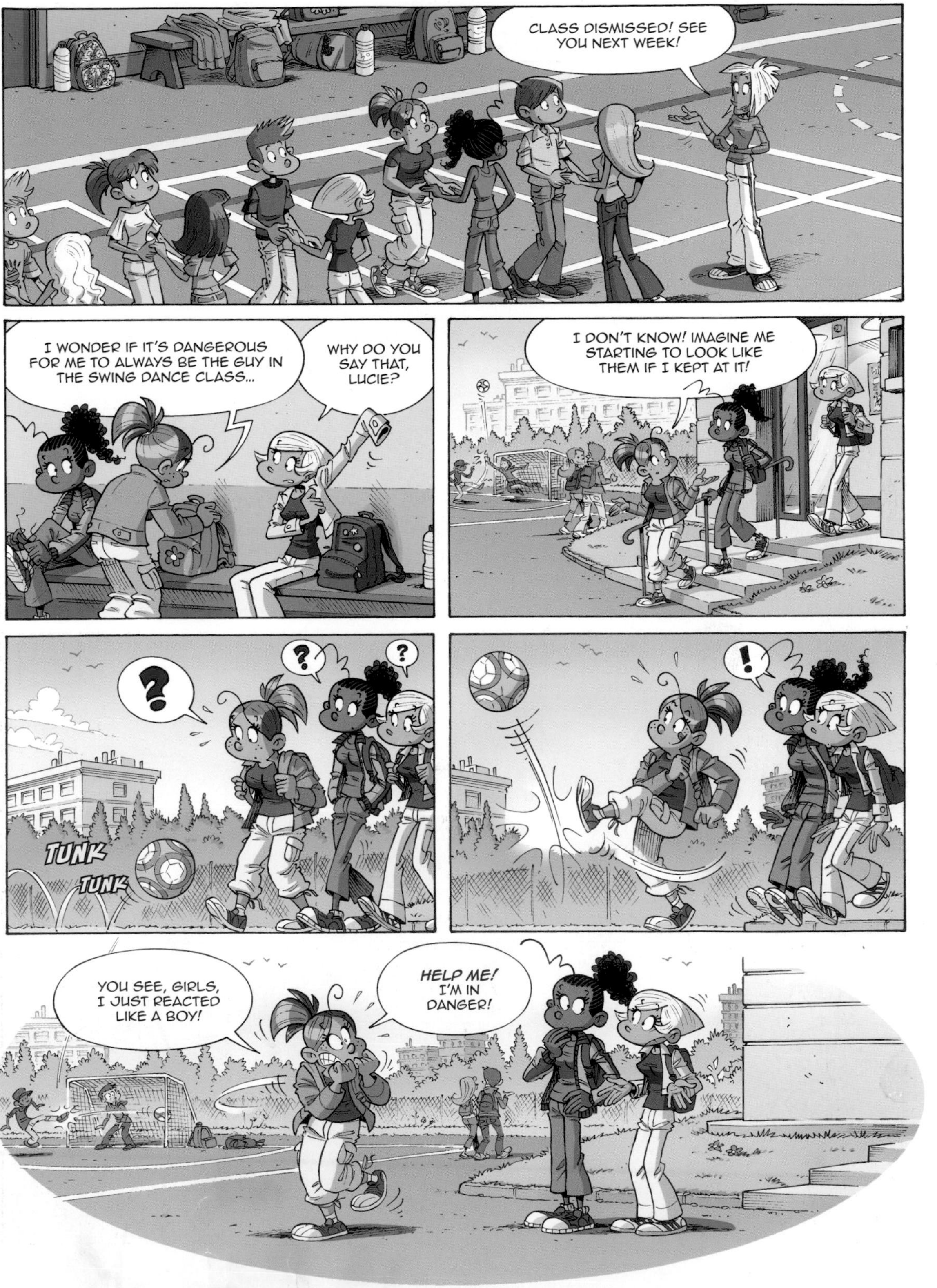
CLASS DISMISSED! SEE YOU NEXT WEEK!
I WONDER IF IT'S DANGEROUS FOR ME TO ALWAYS BE THE GUY IN THE SWING DANCE CLASS...
WHY DO YOU SAY THAT, LUCIE?
I DON'T KNOW! IMAGINE ME STARTING TO LOOK LIKE THEM IF I KEPT AT IT!
?
?
?
TUNK
TUNK
!
YOU SEE, GIRLS, I JUST REACTED LIKE A BOY!
HELP ME! I'M IN DANGER!

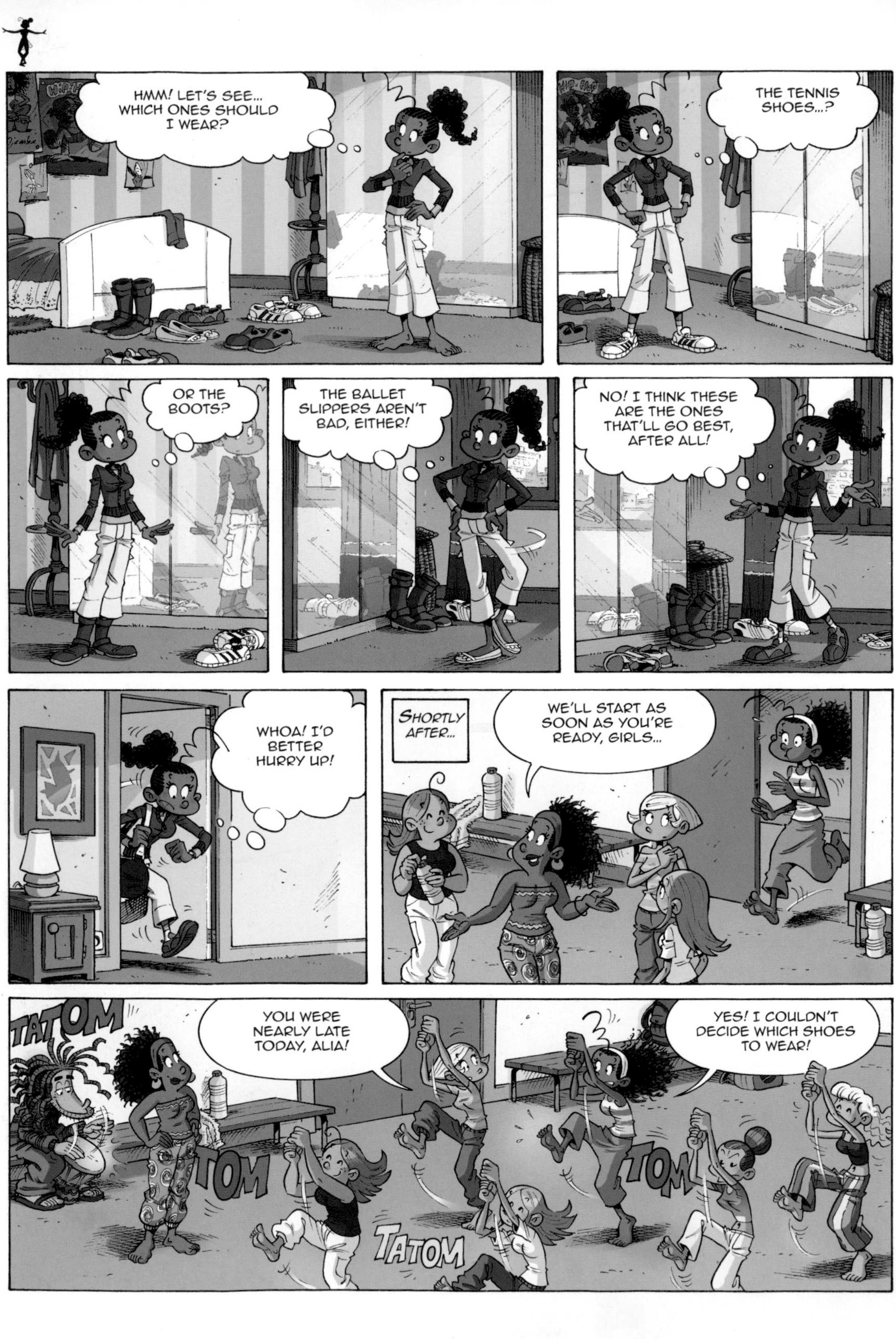

HMM! LET'S SEE... WHICH ONES SHOULD I WEAR?
THE TENNIS SHOES...?
OR THE BOOTS?
THE BALLET SLIPPERS AREN'T BAD, EITHER!
NO! I THINK THESE ARE THE ONES THAT'LL GO BEST, AFTER ALL!
WHOA! I'D BETTER HURRY UP!
SHORTLY AFTER...
WE'LL START AS SOON AS YOU'RE READY, GIRLS...
TATOM
YOU WERE NEARLY LATE TODAY, ALIA!
YES! I COULDN'T DECIDE WHICH SHOES TO WEAR!
TOM
TOM
TATOM

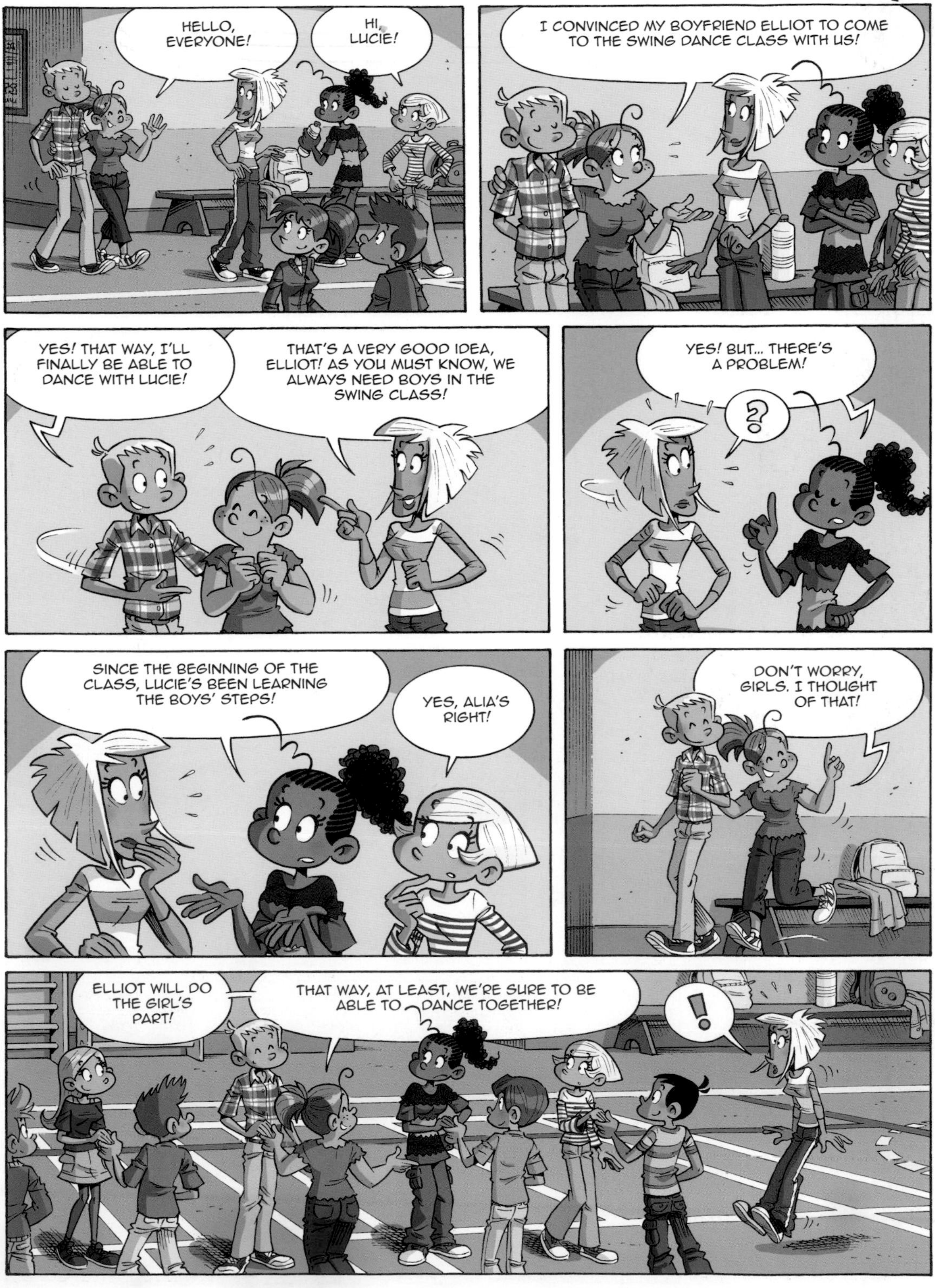
HELLO, EVERYONE!
HI, LUCIE!
I CONVINCED MY BOYFRIEND ELLIOT TO COME TO THE SWING DANCE CLASS WITH US!
YES! THAT WAY, I'LL FINALLY BE ABLE TO DANCE WITH LUCIE!
THAT'S A VERY GOOD IDEA, ELLIOT! AS YOU MUST KNOW, WE ALWAYS NEED BOYS IN THE SWING CLASS!
YES! BUT... THERE'S A PROBLEM!
?
SINCE THE BEGINNING OF THE CLASS, LUCIE'S BEEN LEARNING THE BOYS' STEPS!
YES, ALIA'S RIGHT!
DON'T WORRY, GIRLS. I THOUGHT OF THAT!
ELLIOT WILL DO THE GIRL'S PART!
THAT WAY, AT LEAST, WE'RE SURE TO BE ABLE TO DANCE TOGETHER!
!

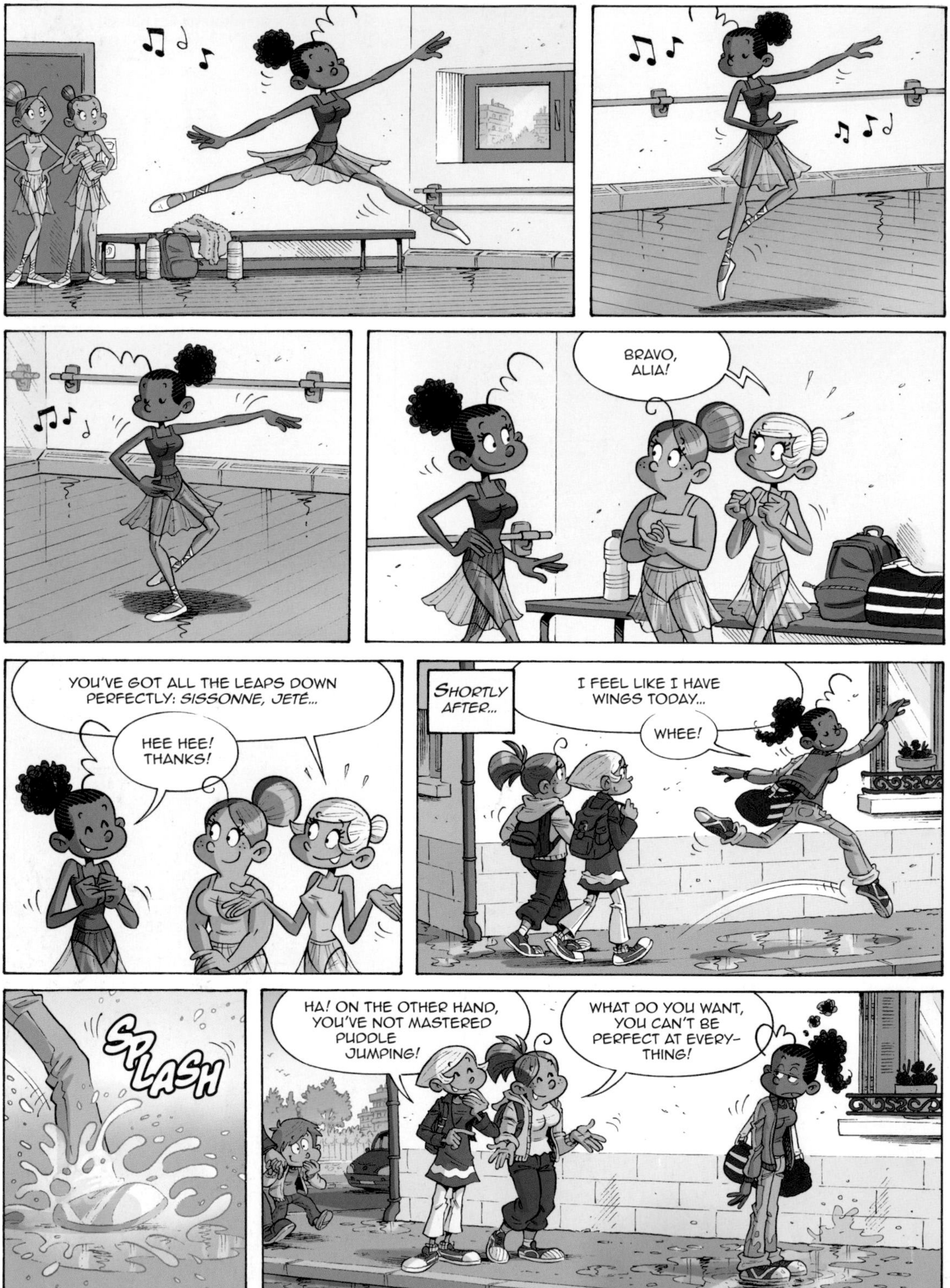
BRAVO, ALIA!
YOU'VE GOT ALL THE LEAPS DOWN PERFECTLY: *SISSONNE, JETÉ*...
HEE HEE! THANKS!
SHORTLY AFTER...
I FEEL LIKE I HAVE WINGS TODAY...
WHEE!
SPLASH
HA! ON THE OTHER HAND, YOU'VE NOT MASTERED PUDDLE JUMPING!
WHAT DO YOU WANT, YOU CAN'T BE PERFECT AT EVERY-THING!

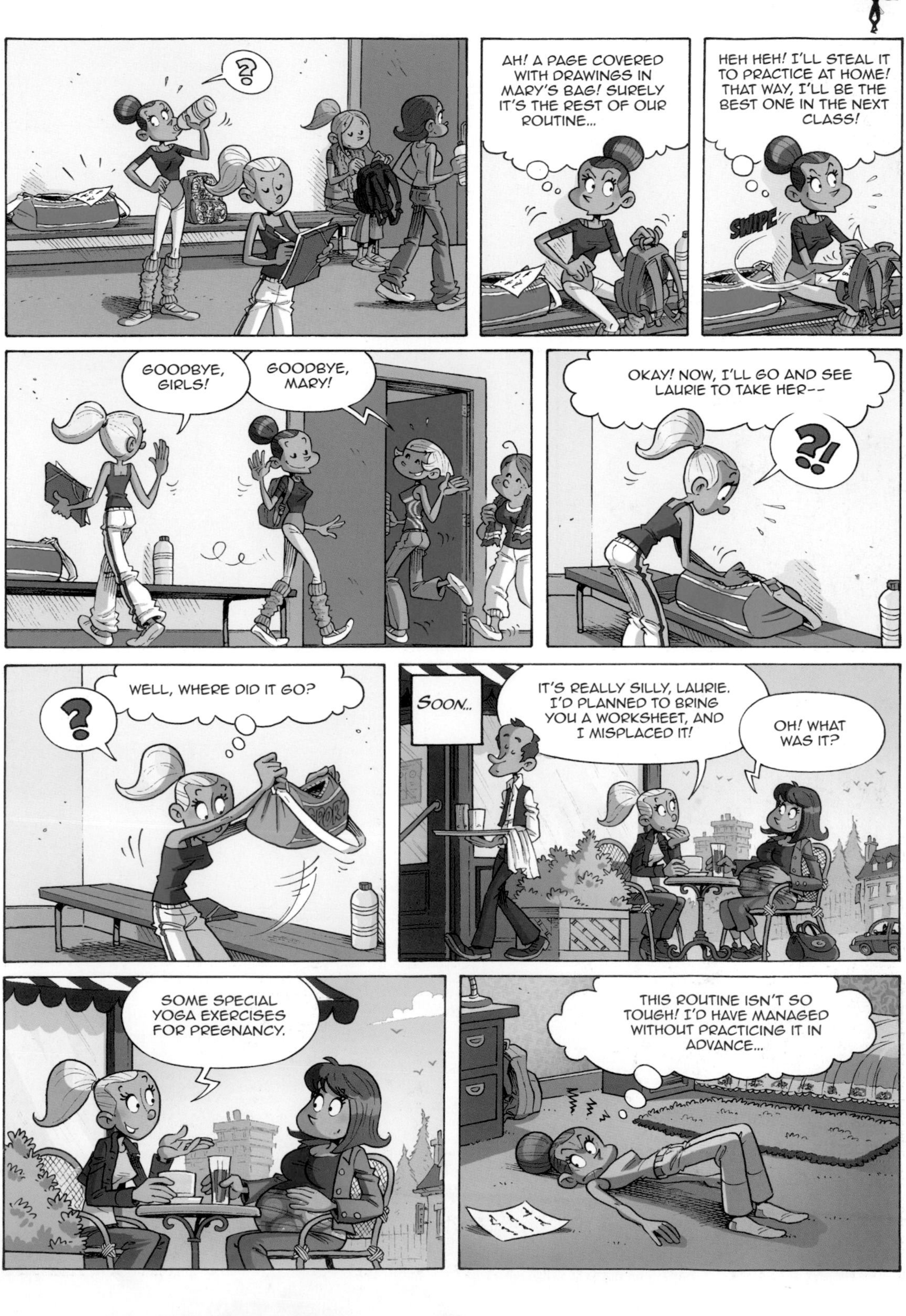
?
AH! A PAGE COVERED WITH DRAWINGS IN MARY'S BAG! SURELY IT'S THE REST OF OUR ROUTINE...
HEH HEH! I'LL STEAL IT TO PRACTICE AT HOME! THAT WAY, I'LL BE THE BEST ONE IN THE NEXT CLASS!
SWIPE
GOODBYE, GIRLS!
GOODBYE, MARY!
OKAY! NOW, I'LL GO AND SEE LAURIE TO TAKE HER--
?!
WELL, WHERE DID IT GO?
?
SOON...
IT'S REALLY SILLY, LAURIE. I'D PLANNED TO BRING YOU A WORKSHEET, AND I MISPLACED IT!
OH! WHAT WAS IT?
SOME SPECIAL YOGA EXERCISES FOR PREGNANCY.
THIS ROUTINE ISN'T SO TOUGH! I'D HAVE MANAGED WITHOUT PRACTICING IT IN ADVANCE...

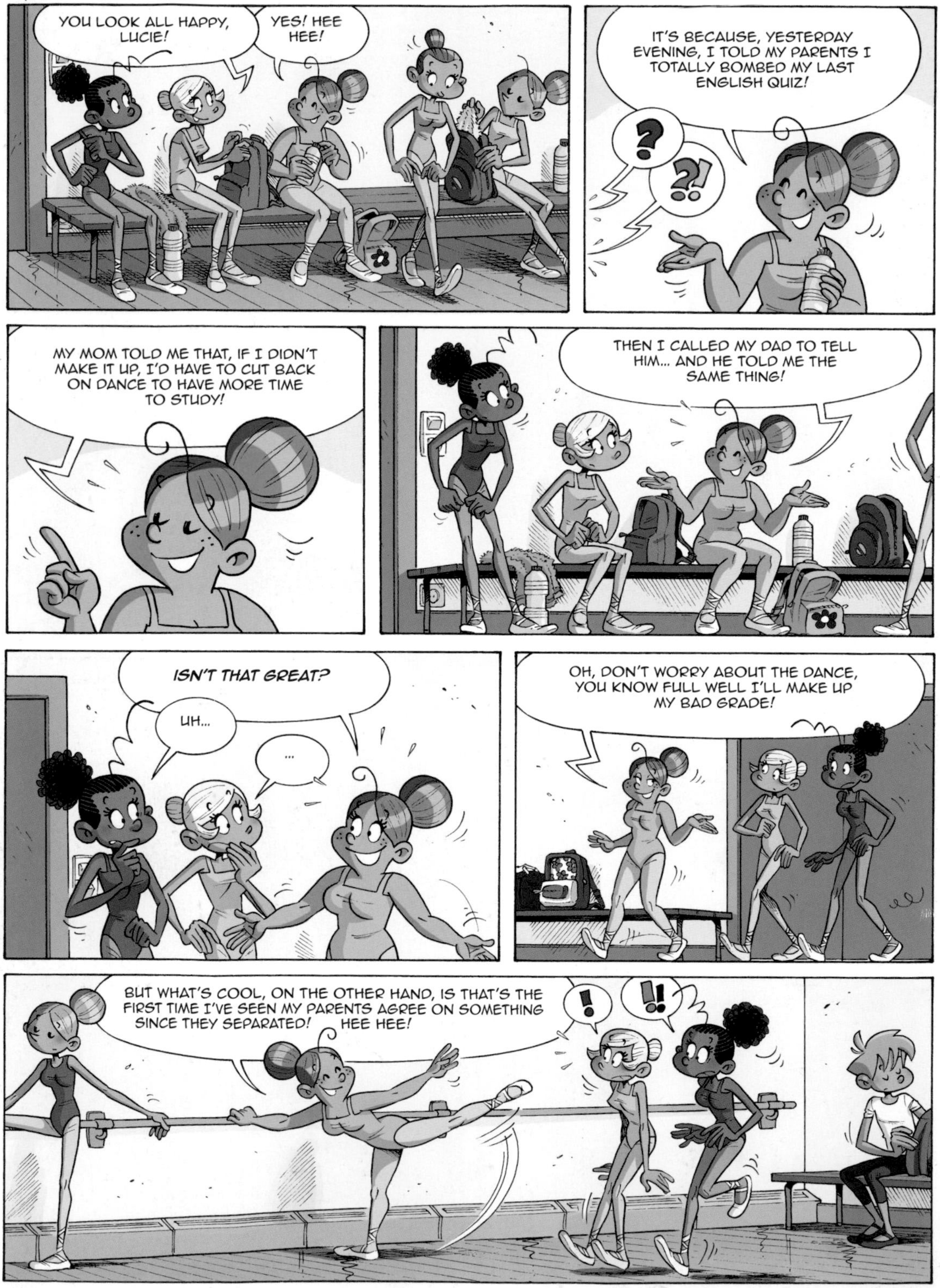
YOU LOOK ALL HAPPY, LUCIE!
YES! HEE HEE!
IT'S BECAUSE, YESTERDAY EVENING, I TOLD MY PARENTS I TOTALLY BOMBED MY LAST ENGLISH QUIZ!
?
?!
MY MOM TOLD ME THAT, IF I DIDN'T MAKE IT UP, I'D HAVE TO CUT BACK ON DANCE TO HAVE MORE TIME TO STUDY!
THEN I CALLED MY DAD TO TELL HIM... AND HE TOLD ME THE SAME THING!
ISN'T THAT GREAT?
UH...
...
OH, DON'T WORRY ABOUT THE DANCE, YOU KNOW FULL WELL I'LL MAKE UP MY BAD GRADE!
BUT WHAT'S COOL, ON THE OTHER HAND, IS THAT'S THE FIRST TIME I'VE SEEN MY PARENTS AGREE ON SOMETHING SINCE THEY SEPARATED! HEE HEE!
!
!!

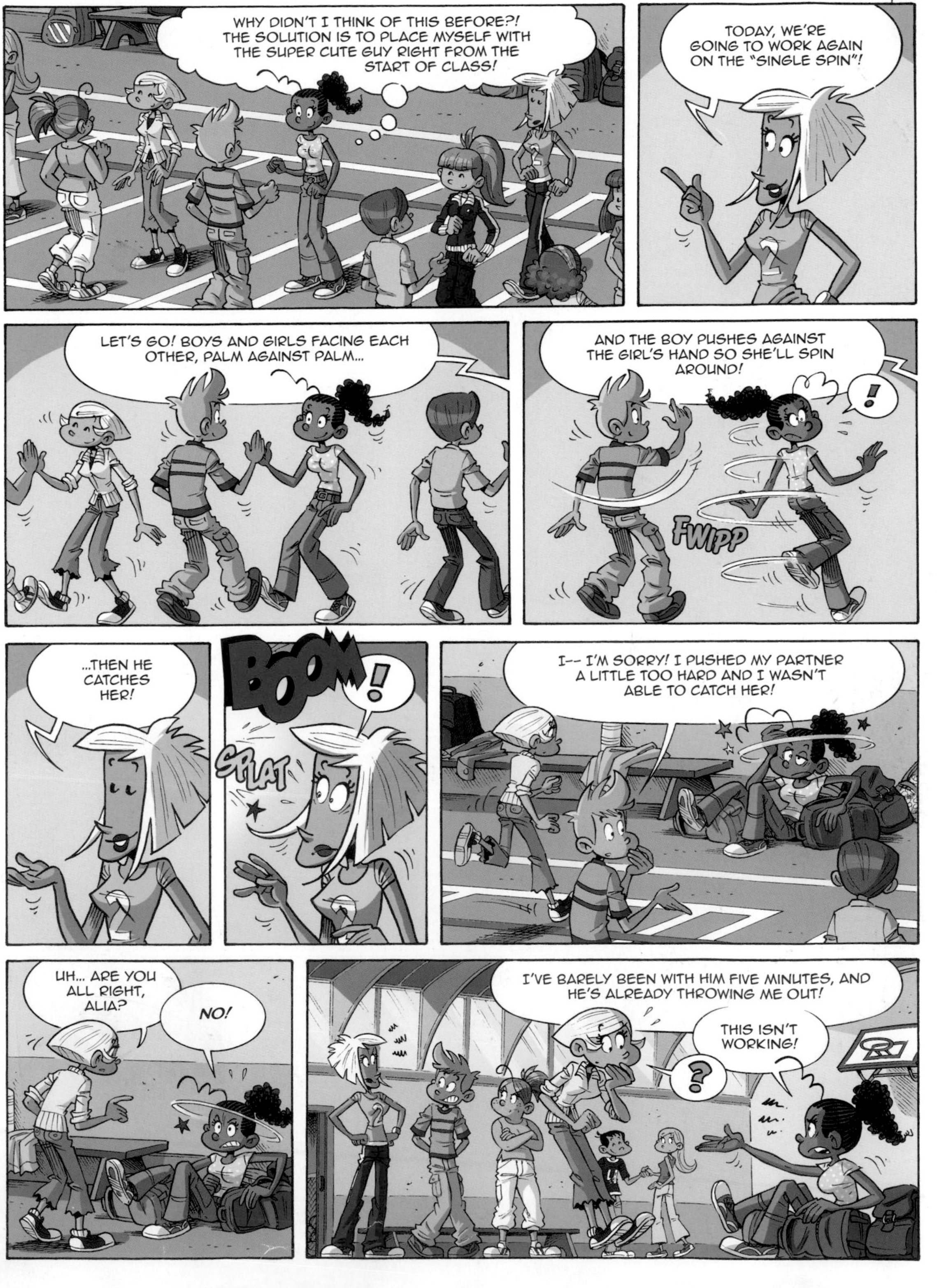
WHY DIDN'T I THINK OF THIS BEFORE?! THE SOLUTION IS TO PLACE MYSELF WITH THE SUPER CUTE GUY RIGHT FROM THE START OF CLASS!
TODAY, WE'RE GOING TO WORK AGAIN ON THE "SINGLE SPIN"!
LET'S GO! BOYS AND GIRLS FACING EACH OTHER, PALM AGAINST PALM...
AND THE BOY PUSHES AGAINST THE GIRL'S HAND SO SHE'LL SPIN AROUND!
!
FWIPP
...THEN HE CATCHES HER!
BOOM
!
SPLAT
I-- I'M SORRY! I PUSHED MY PARTNER A LITTLE TOO HARD AND I WASN'T ABLE TO CATCH HER!
UH... ARE YOU ALL RIGHT, ALIA?
NO!
I'VE BARELY BEEN WITH HIM FIVE MINUTES, AND HE'S ALREADY THROWING ME OUT!
?
THIS ISN'T WORKING!

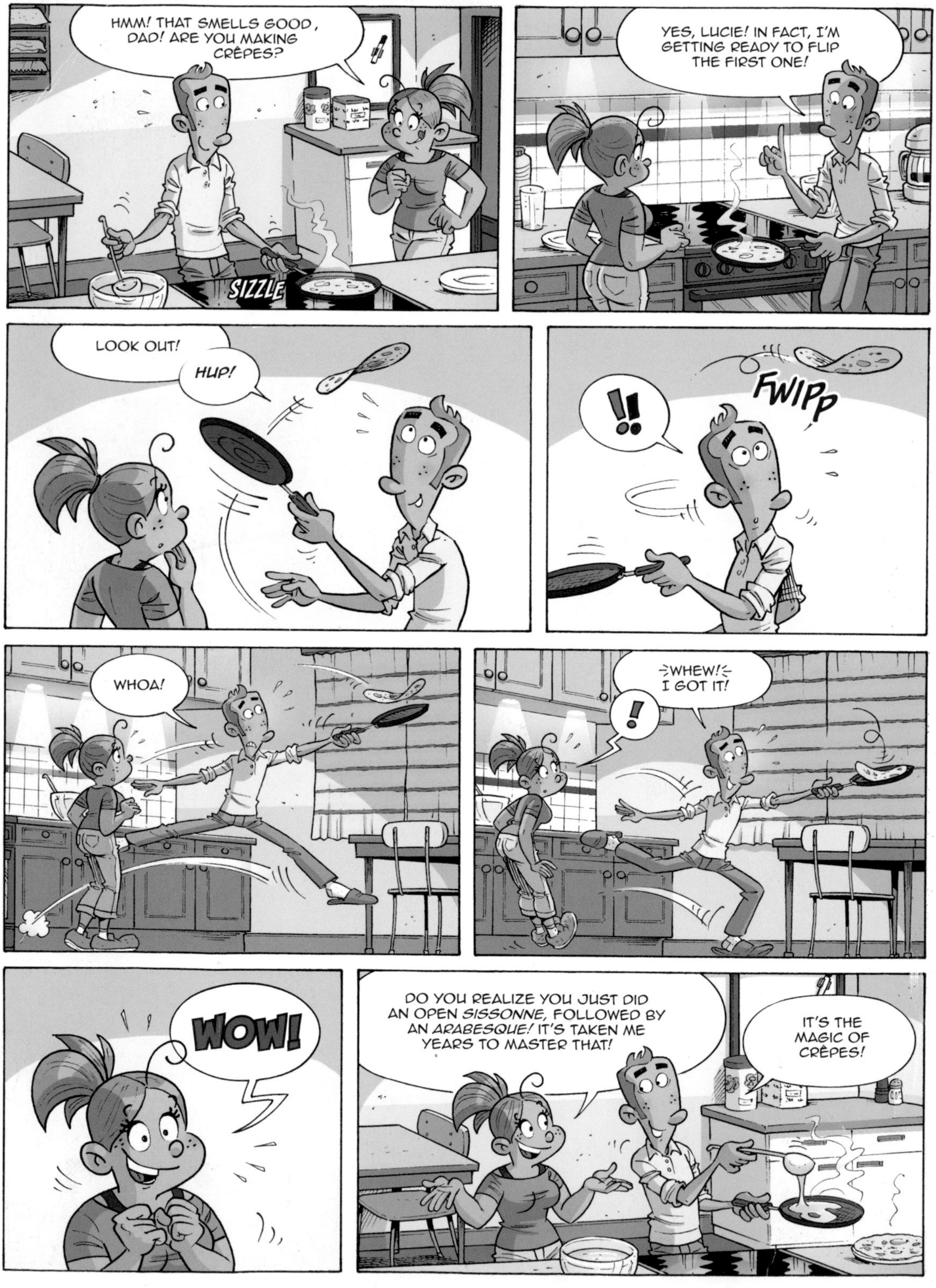
HMM! THAT SMELLS GOOD, DAD! ARE YOU MAKING CRÊPES?
SIZZLE
YES, LUCIE! IN FACT, I'M GETTING READY TO FLIP THE FIRST ONE!
LOOK OUT!
HUP!
!!
FWIPP
WHOA!
!
-WHEW!- I GOT IT!
WOW!
DO YOU REALIZE YOU JUST DID AN OPEN *SISSONNE*, FOLLOWED BY AN *ARABESQUE*! IT'S TAKEN ME YEARS TO MASTER THAT!
IT'S THE MAGIC OF CRÊPES!

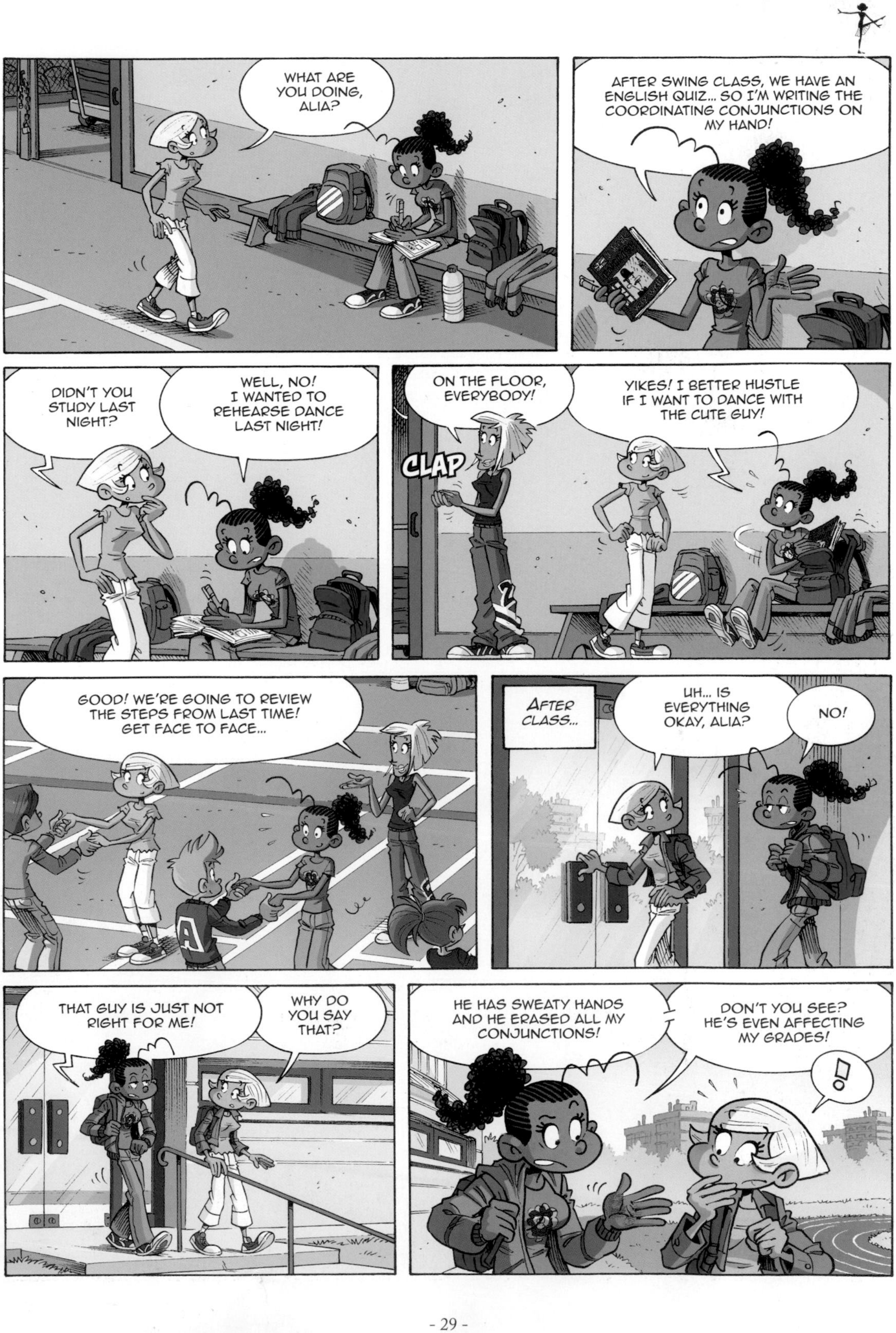
WHAT ARE YOU DOING, ALIA?
AFTER SWING CLASS, WE HAVE AN ENGLISH QUIZ... SO I'M WRITING THE COORDINATING CONJUNCTIONS ON MY HAND!
DIDN'T YOU STUDY LAST NIGHT?
WELL, NO! I WANTED TO REHEARSE DANCE LAST NIGHT!
ON THE FLOOR, EVERYBODY!
CLAP
YIKES! I BETTER HUSTLE IF I WANT TO DANCE WITH THE CUTE GUY!
GOOD! WE'RE GOING TO REVIEW THE STEPS FROM LAST TIME! GET FACE TO FACE...
AFTER CLASS...
UH... IS EVERYTHING OKAY, ALIA?
NO!
THAT GUY IS JUST NOT RIGHT FOR ME!
WHY DO YOU SAY THAT?
HE HAS SWEATY HANDS AND HE ERASED ALL MY CONJUNCTIONS!
DON'T YOU SEE? HE'S EVEN AFFECTING MY GRADES!
!

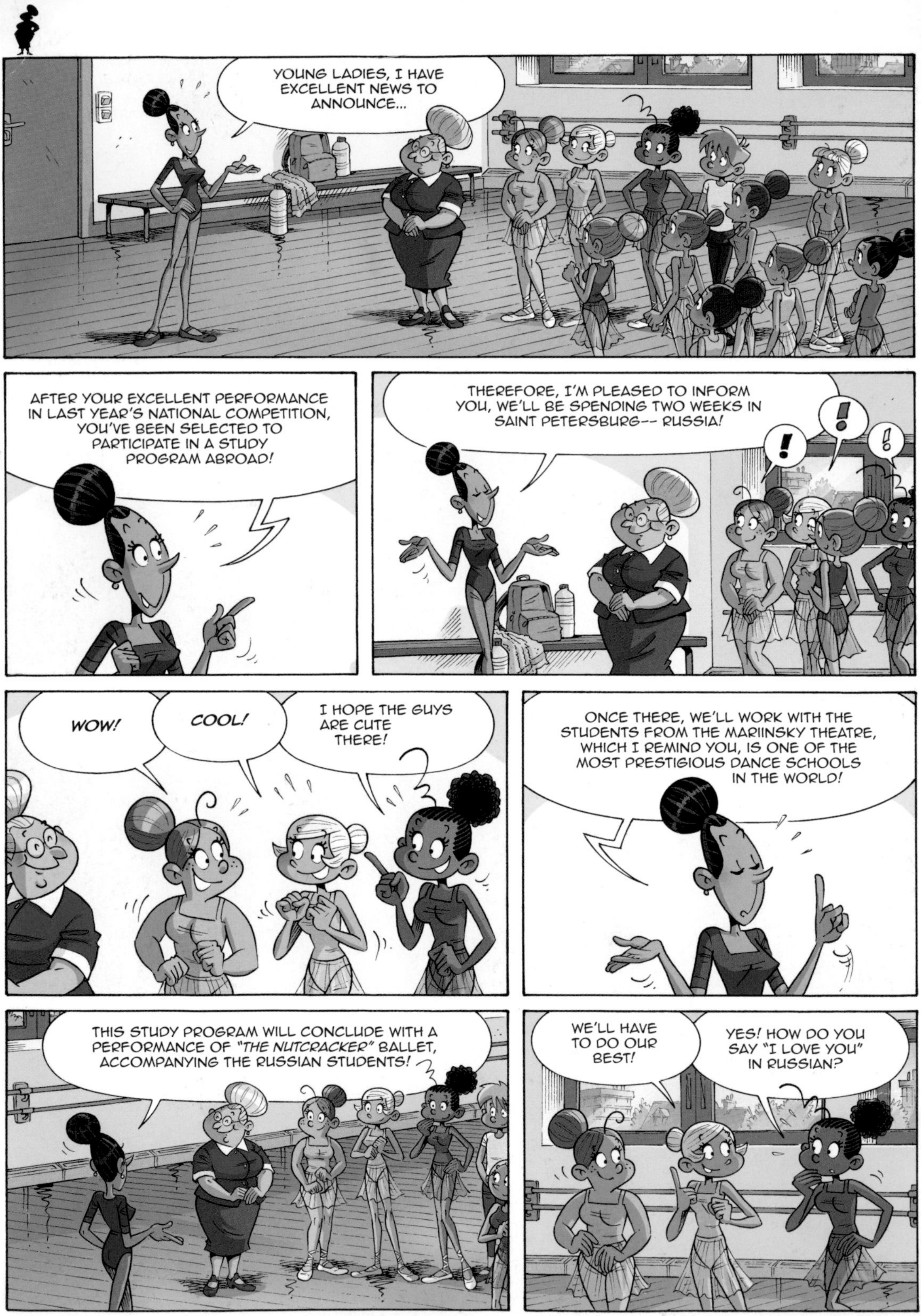
YOUNG LADIES, I HAVE EXCELLENT NEWS TO ANNOUNCE...
AFTER YOUR EXCELLENT PERFORMANCE IN LAST YEAR'S NATIONAL COMPETITION, YOU'VE BEEN SELECTED TO PARTICIPATE IN A STUDY PROGRAM ABROAD!
THEREFORE, I'M PLEASED TO INFORM YOU, WE'LL BE SPENDING TWO WEEKS IN SAINT PETERSBURG-- RUSSIA!
!
!
!
WOW!
COOL!
I HOPE THE GUYS ARE CUTE THERE!
ONCE THERE, WE'LL WORK WITH THE STUDENTS FROM THE MARIINSKY THEATRE, WHICH I REMIND YOU, IS ONE OF THE MOST PRESTIGIOUS DANCE SCHOOLS IN THE WORLD!
THIS STUDY PROGRAM WILL CONCLUDE WITH A PERFORMANCE OF "THE NUTCRACKER" BALLET, ACCOMPANYING THE RUSSIAN STUDENTS!
WE'LL HAVE TO DO OUR BEST!
YES! HOW DO YOU SAY "I LOVE YOU" IN RUSSIAN?

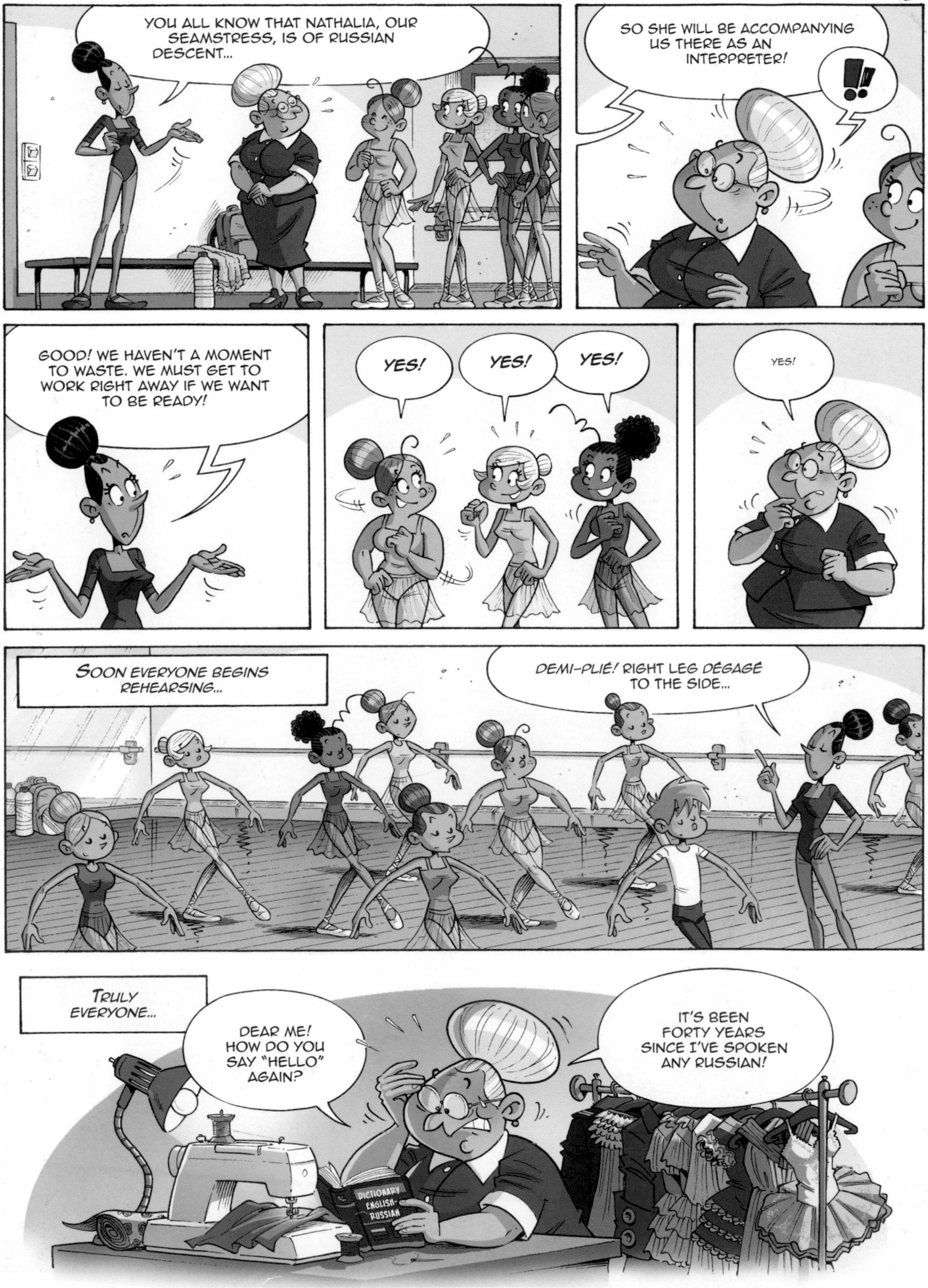

YOU ALL KNOW THAT NATHALIA, OUR SEAMSTRESS, IS OF RUSSIAN DESCENT...
SO SHE WILL BE ACCOMPANYING US THERE AS AN INTERPRETER!
!!
GOOD! WE HAVEN'T A MOMENT TO WASTE. WE MUST GET TO WORK RIGHT AWAY IF WE WANT TO BE READY!
YES!
YES!
YES!
YES!
SOON EVERYONE BEGINS REHEARSING...
DEMI-PLIÉ! RIGHT LEG DÉGAGÉ TO THE SIDE...
TRULY EVERYONE...
DEAR ME! HOW DO YOU SAY "HELLO" AGAIN?
IT'S BEEN FORTY YEARS SINCE I'VE SPOKEN ANY RUSSIAN!
DICTIONARY ENGLISH-RUSSIAN

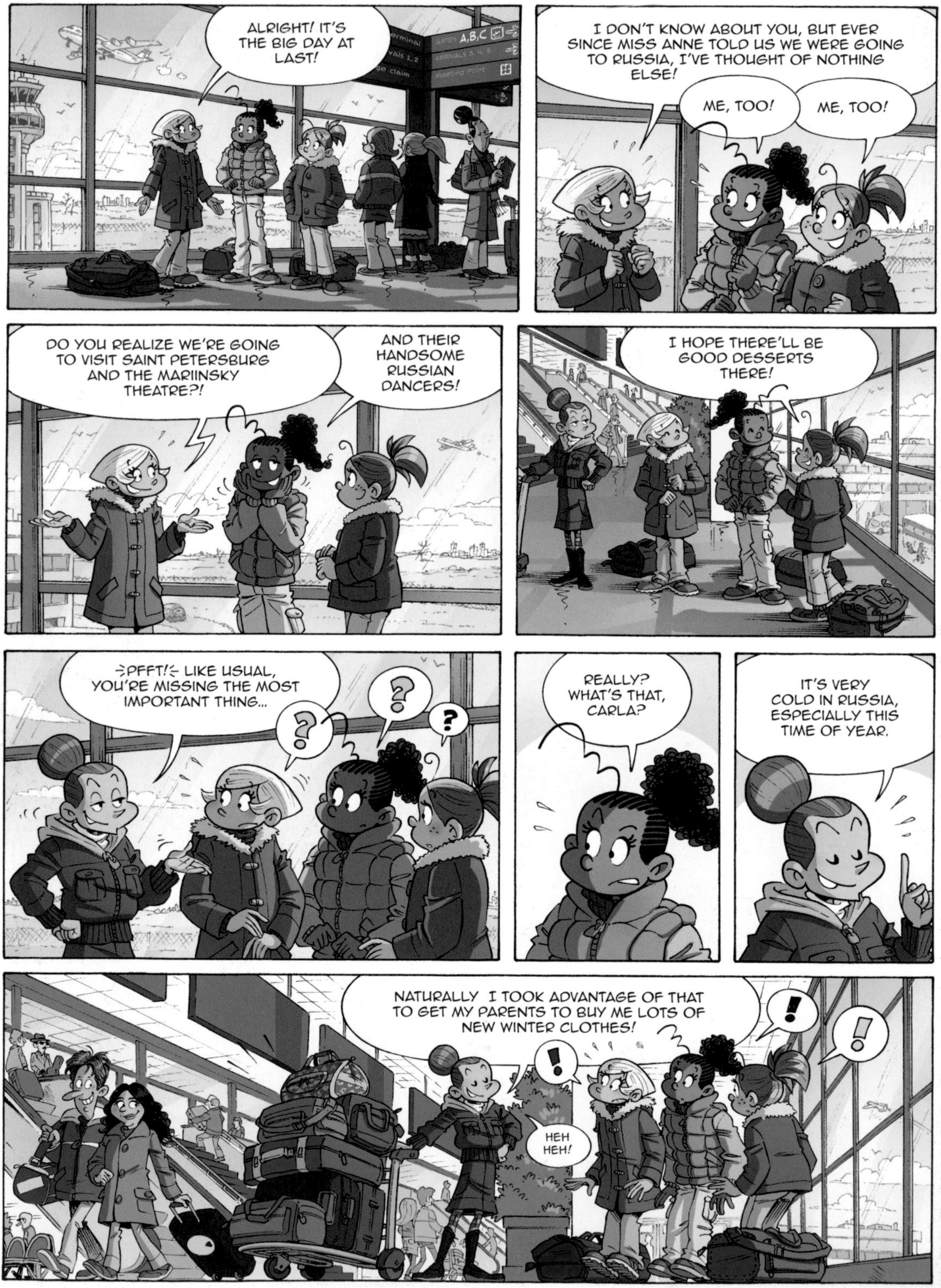
ALRIGHT! IT'S THE BIG DAY AT LAST!
I DON'T KNOW ABOUT YOU, BUT EVER SINCE MISS ANNE TOLD US WE WERE GOING TO RUSSIA, I'VE THOUGHT OF NOTHING ELSE!
ME, TOO!
ME, TOO!
DO YOU REALIZE WE'RE GOING TO VISIT SAINT PETERSBURG AND THE MARIINSKY THEATRE?!
AND THEIR HANDSOME RUSSIAN DANCERS!
I HOPE THERE'LL BE GOOD DESSERTS THERE!
PFFT! LIKE USUAL, YOU'RE MISSING THE MOST IMPORTANT THING...
?
?
?
REALLY? WHAT'S THAT, CARLA?
IT'S VERY COLD IN RUSSIA, ESPECIALLY THIS TIME OF YEAR.
NATURALLY I TOOK ADVANTAGE OF THAT TO GET MY PARENTS TO BUY ME LOTS OF NEW WINTER CLOTHES!
!
!
!
HEH HEH!

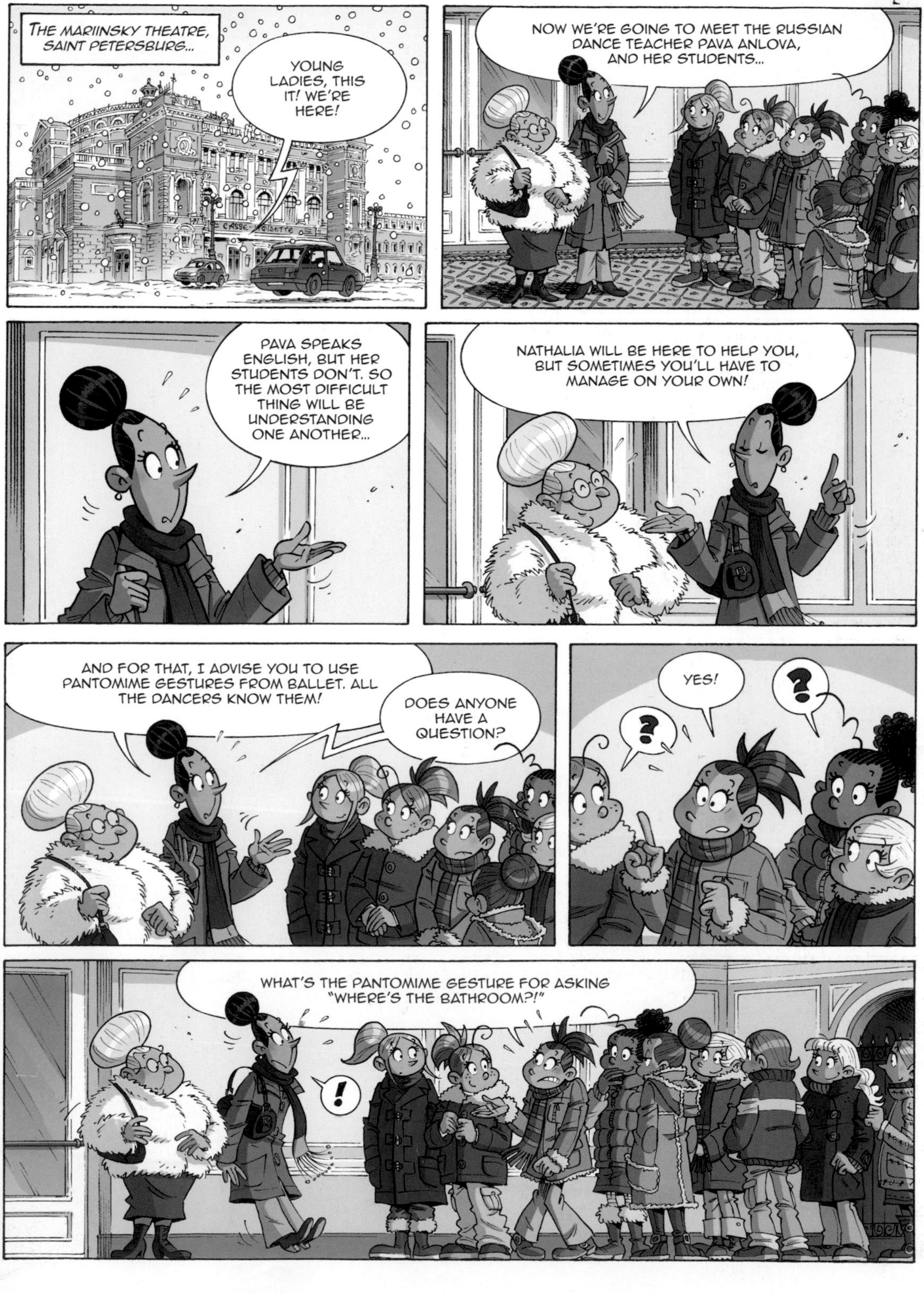
THE MARIINSKY THEATRE, SAINT PETERSBURG...
YOUNG LADIES, THIS IT! WE'RE HERE!
NOW WE'RE GOING TO MEET THE RUSSIAN DANCE TEACHER PAVA ANLOVA, AND HER STUDENTS...
PAVA SPEAKS ENGLISH, BUT HER STUDENTS DON'T. SO THE MOST DIFFICULT THING WILL BE UNDERSTANDING ONE ANOTHER...
NATHALIA WILL BE HERE TO HELP YOU, BUT SOMETIMES YOU'LL HAVE TO MANAGE ON YOUR OWN!
AND FOR THAT, I ADVISE YOU TO USE PANTOMIME GESTURES FROM BALLET. ALL THE DANCERS KNOW THEM!
DOES ANYONE HAVE A QUESTION?
?
YES!
?
WHAT'S THE PANTOMIME GESTURE FOR ASKING "WHERE'S THE BATHROOM?!"
!

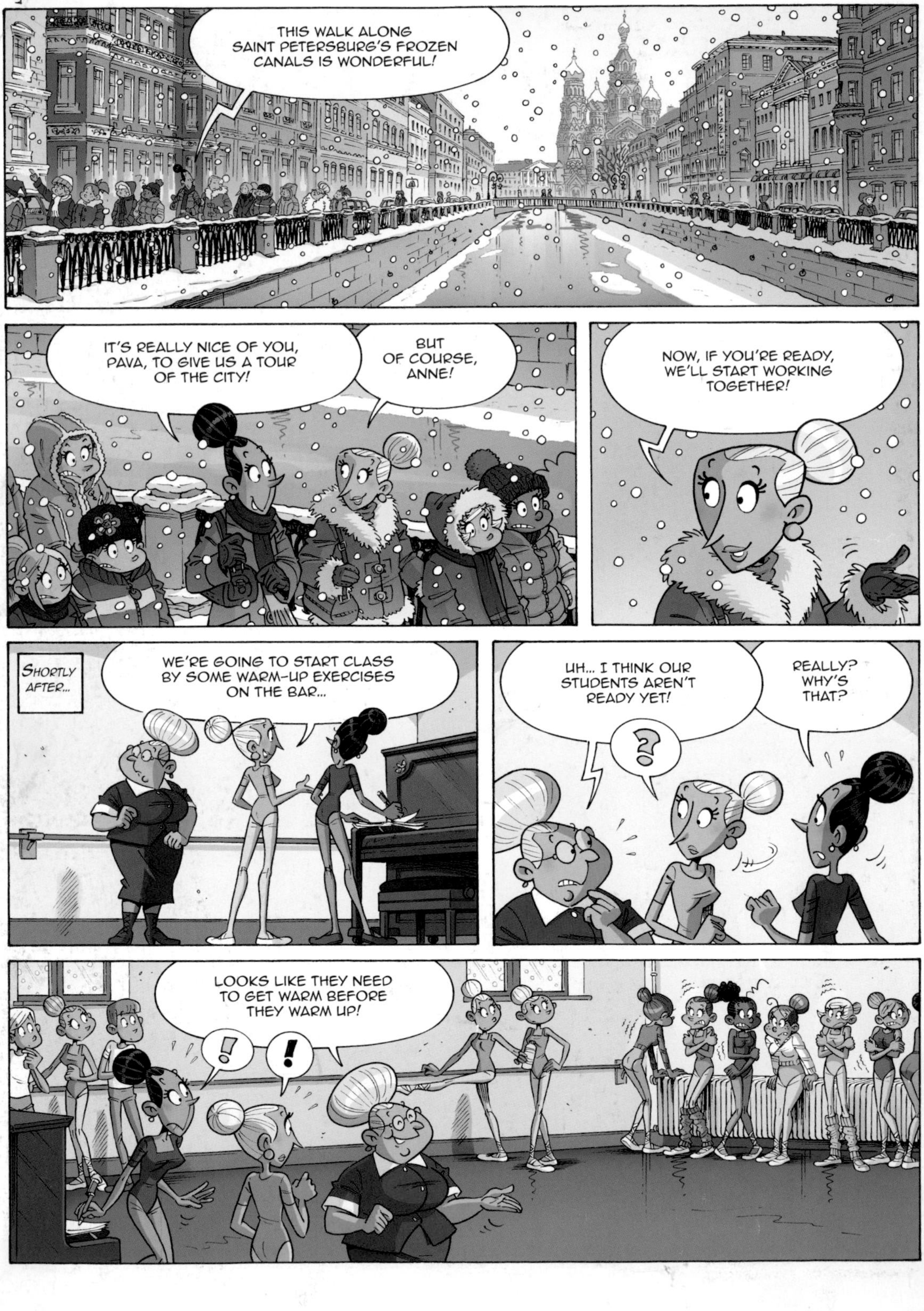
THIS WALK ALONG SAINT PETERSBURG'S FROZEN CANALS IS WONDERFUL!
IT'S REALLY NICE OF YOU, PAVA, TO GIVE US A TOUR OF THE CITY!
BUT OF COURSE, ANNE!
NOW, IF YOU'RE READY, WE'LL START WORKING TOGETHER!
SHORTLY AFTER...
WE'RE GOING TO START CLASS BY SOME WARM-UP EXERCISES ON THE BAR...
UH... I THINK OUR STUDENTS AREN'T READY YET!
?
REALLY? WHY'S THAT?
LOOKS LIKE THEY NEED TO GET WARM BEFORE THEY WARM UP!
!
!

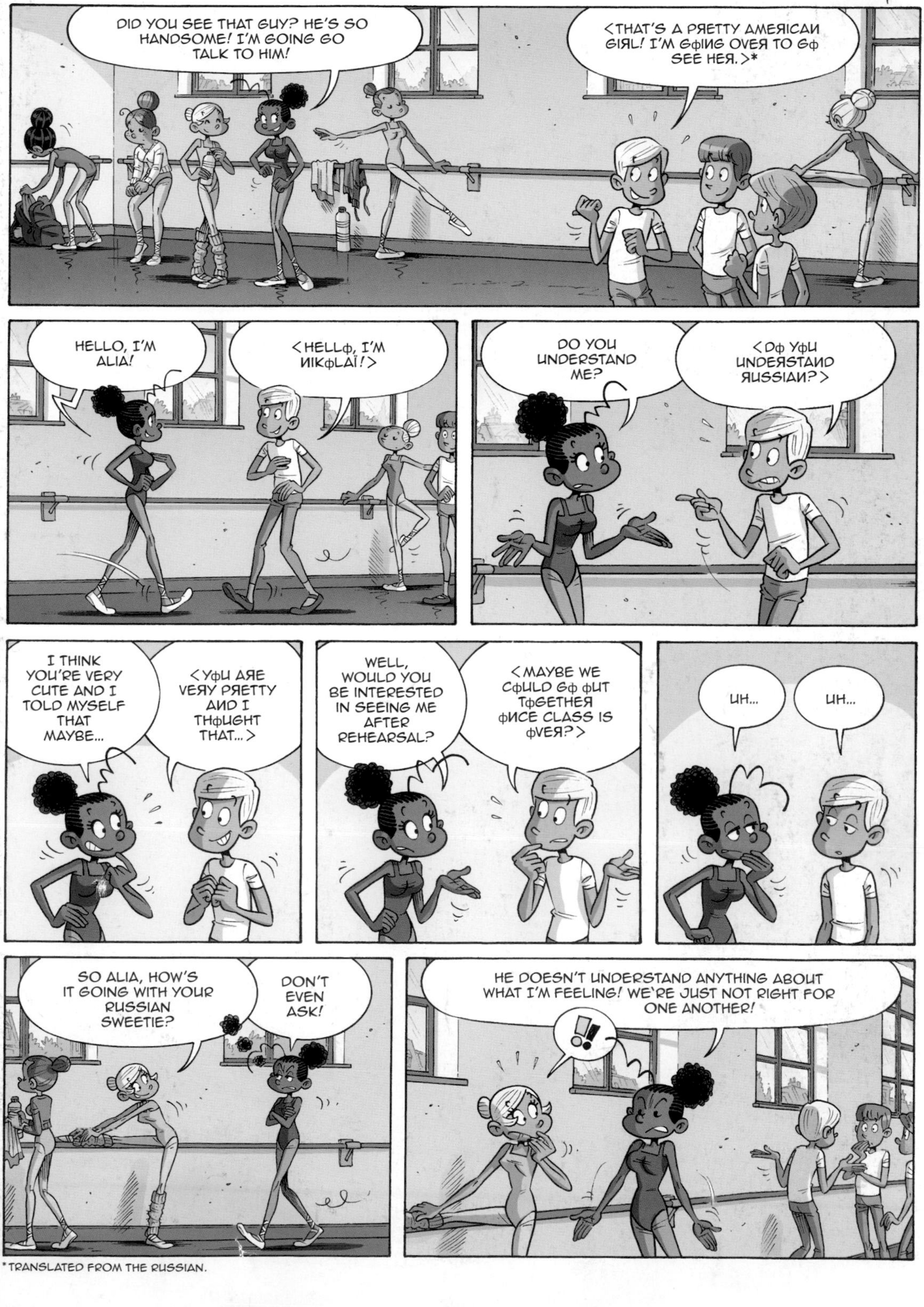
DID YOU SEE THAT GUY? HE'S SO HANDSOME! I'M GOING GO TALK TO HIM!
<THAT'S A PЯETTY AMEЯICAИ GIЯL! I'M GфIИG OVEЯ TO Gф SEE HEЯ.>*
HELLO, I'M ALIA!
<HELLф, I'M ИIKфLAÏ!>
DO YOU UNDERSTAND ME?
<Dф YфU UИDEЯSTAИD ЯUSSIAИ?>
I THINK YOU'RE VERY CUTE AND I TOLD MYSELF THAT MAYBE...
<YфU AЯE VEЯY PЯETTY AИD I THфUGHT THAT...>
WELL, WOULD YOU BE INTERESTED IN SEEING ME AFTER REHEARSAL?
<MAYBE WE CфULD Gф фUT TфGETHEЯ фИCE CLASS IS фVEЯ?>
UH...
UH...
SO ALIA, HOW'S IT GOING WITH YOUR RUSSIAN SWEETIE?
DON'T EVEN ASK!
HE DOESN'T UNDERSTAND ANYTHING ABOUT WHAT I'M FEELING! WE'RE JUST NOT RIGHT FOR ONE ANOTHER!

*TRANSLATED FROM THE RUSSIAN.

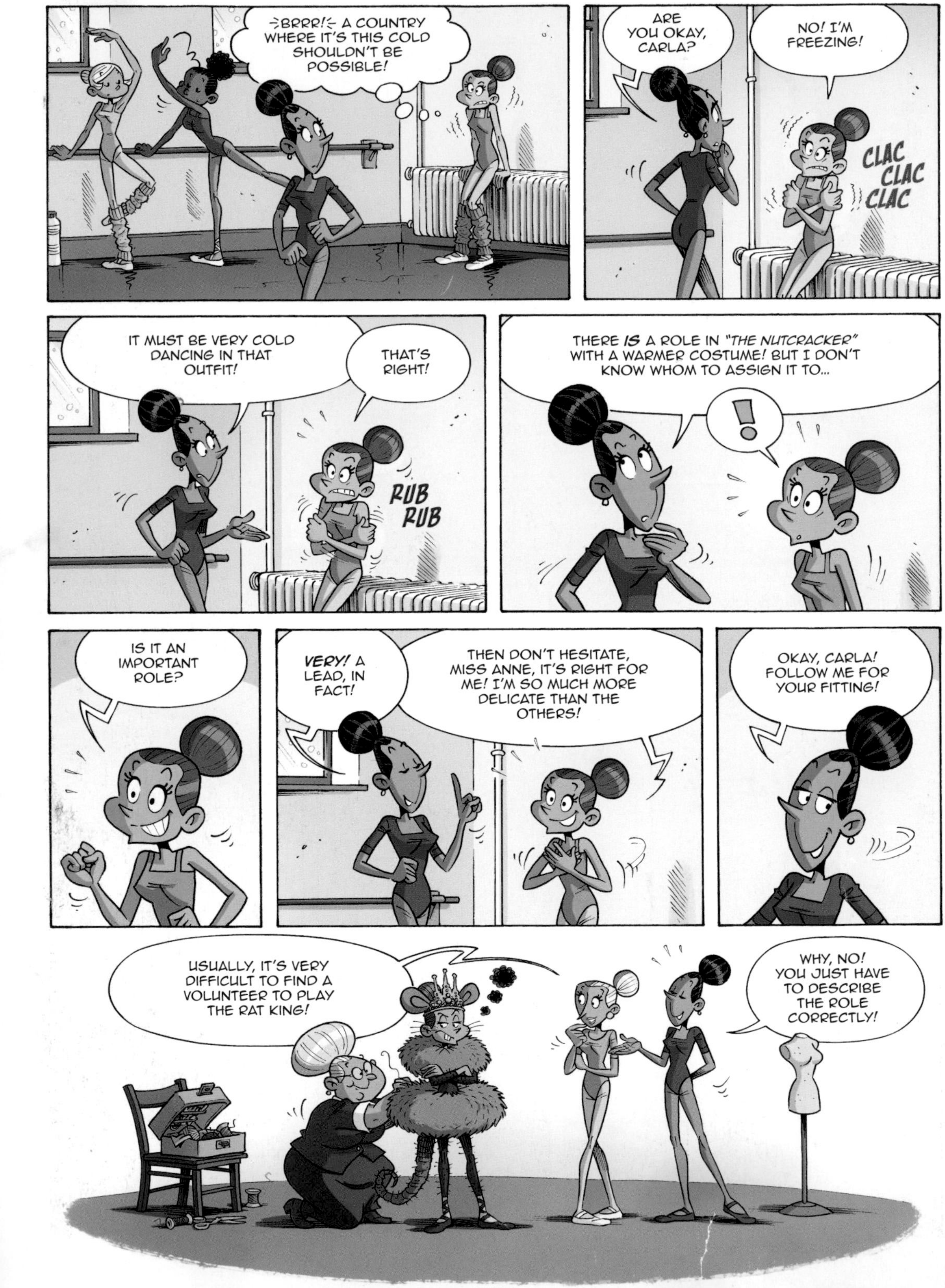
BRRR! A COUNTRY WHERE IT'S THIS COLD SHOULDN'T BE POSSIBLE!
ARE YOU OKAY, CARLA?
NO! I'M FREEZING!
CLAC CLAC CLAC
IT MUST BE VERY COLD DANCING IN THAT OUTFIT!
THAT'S RIGHT!
RUB RUB
THERE *IS* A ROLE IN *"THE NUTCRACKER"* WITH A WARMER COSTUME! BUT I DON'T KNOW WHOM TO ASSIGN IT TO...
!
IS IT AN IMPORTANT ROLE?
VERY! A LEAD, IN FACT!
THEN DON'T HESITATE, MISS ANNE, IT'S RIGHT FOR ME! I'M SO MUCH MORE DELICATE THAN THE OTHERS!
OKAY, CARLA! FOLLOW ME FOR YOUR FITTING!
USUALLY, IT'S VERY DIFFICULT TO FIND A VOLUNTEER TO PLAY THE RAT KING!
WHY, NO! YOU JUST HAVE TO DESCRIBE THE ROLE CORRECTLY!

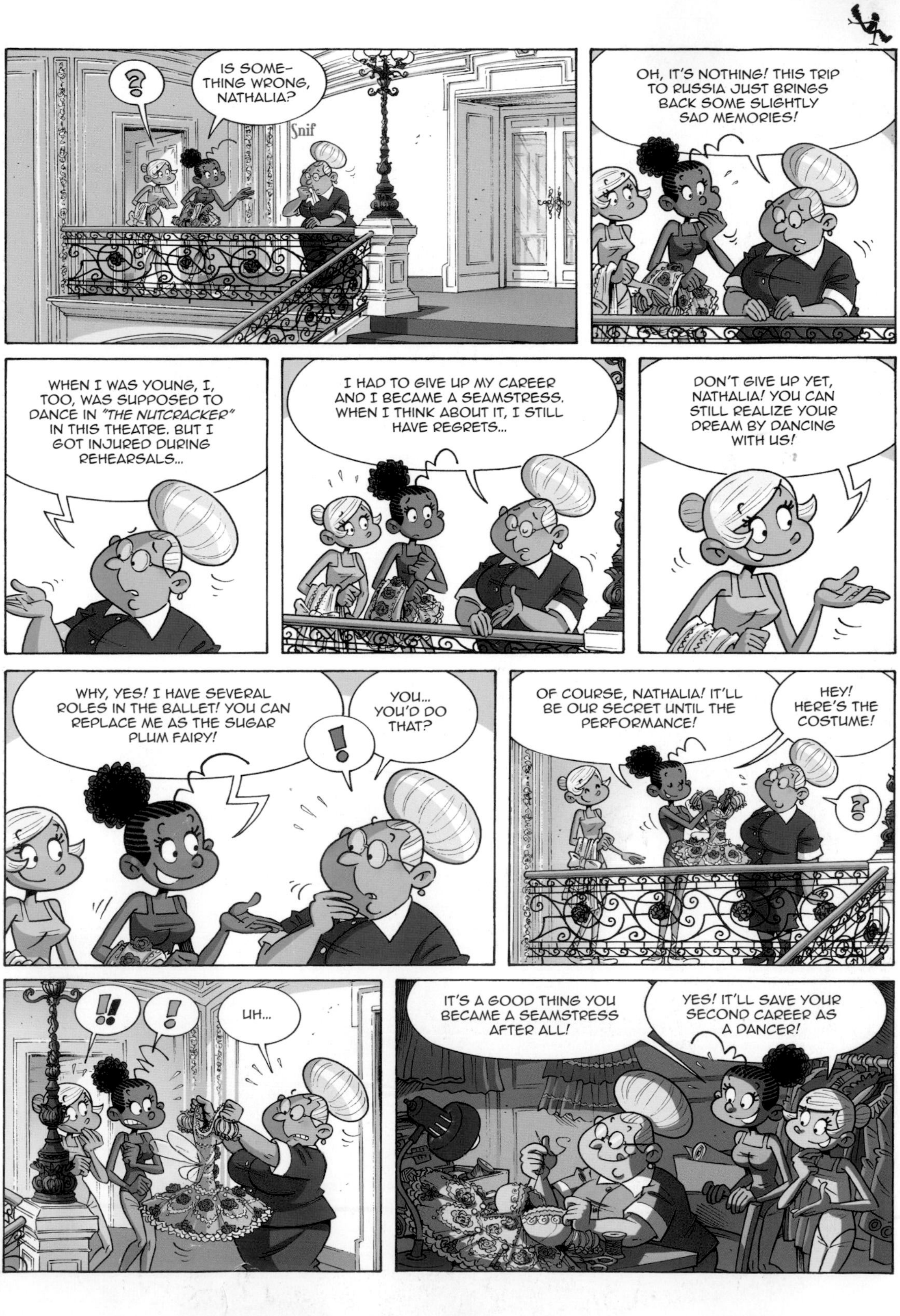
?
IS SOME-THING WRONG, NATHALIA?
Snif
OH, IT'S NOTHING! THIS TRIP TO RUSSIA JUST BRINGS BACK SOME SLIGHTLY SAD MEMORIES!
WHEN I WAS YOUNG, I, TOO, WAS SUPPOSED TO DANCE IN "THE NUTCRACKER" IN THIS THEATRE. BUT I GOT INJURED DURING REHEARSALS...
I HAD TO GIVE UP MY CAREER AND I BECAME A SEAMSTRESS. WHEN I THINK ABOUT IT, I STILL HAVE REGRETS...
DON'T GIVE UP YET, NATHALIA! YOU CAN STILL REALIZE YOUR DREAM BY DANCING WITH US!
WHY, YES! I HAVE SEVERAL ROLES IN THE BALLET! YOU CAN REPLACE ME AS THE SUGAR PLUM FAIRY!
!
YOU... YOU'D DO THAT?
OF COURSE, NATHALIA! IT'LL BE OUR SECRET UNTIL THE PERFORMANCE!
HEY! HERE'S THE COSTUME!
?
!!
!
UH...
IT'S A GOOD THING YOU BECAME A SEAMSTRESS AFTER ALL!
YES! IT'LL SAVE YOUR SECOND CAREER AS A DANCER!

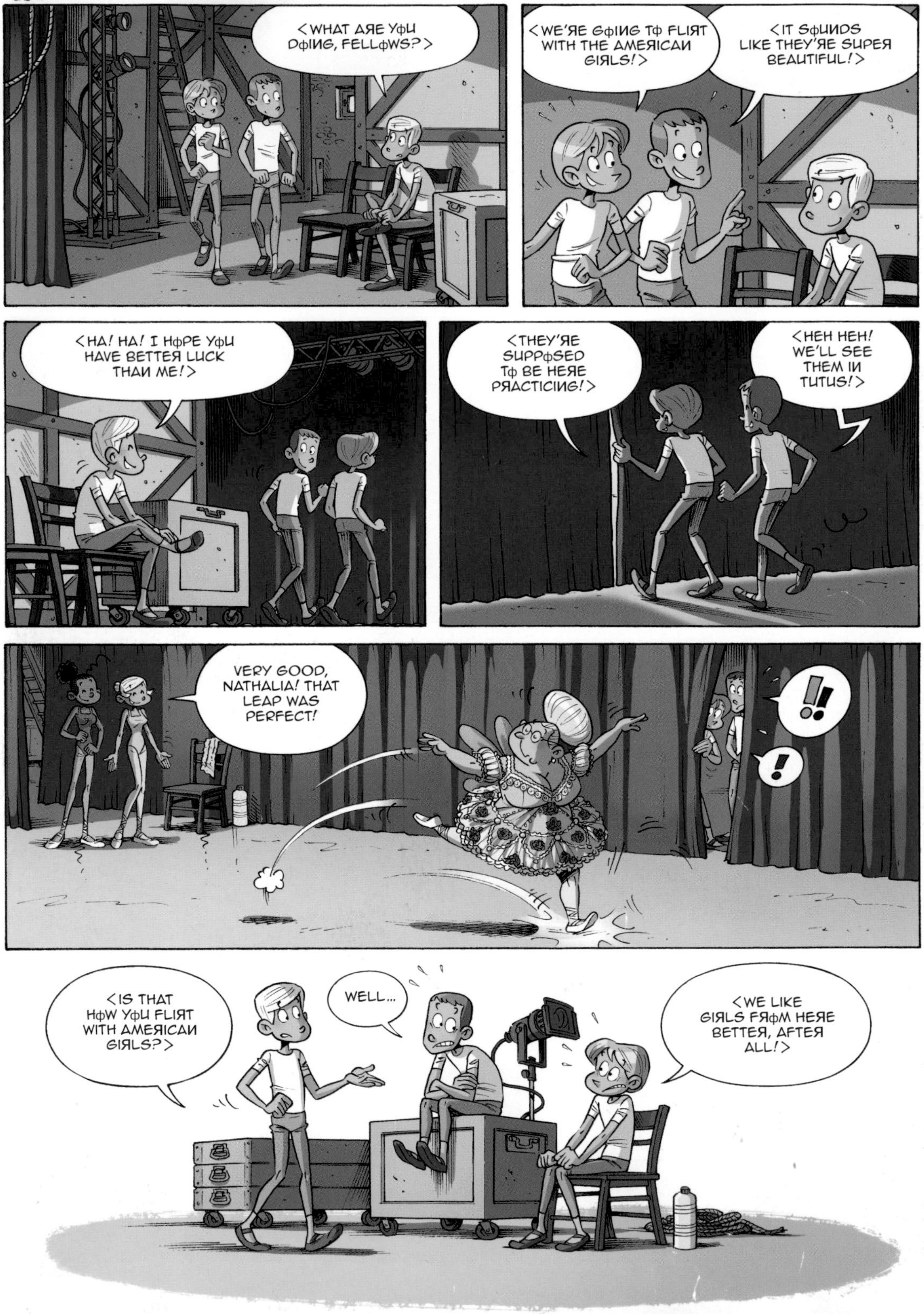
<WHAT ARE YOU DOING, FELLOWS?>
<WE'RE GOING TO FLIRT WITH THE AMERICAN GIRLS!>
<IT SOUNDS LIKE THEY'RE SUPER BEAUTIFUL!>
<HA! HA! I HOPE YOU HAVE BETTER LUCK THAN ME!>
<THEY'RE SUPPOSED TO BE HERE PRACTICING!>
<HEH HEH! WE'LL SEE THEM IN TUTUS!>
VERY GOOD, NATHALIA! THAT LEAP WAS PERFECT!
!!
!
<IS THAT HOW YOU FLIRT WITH AMERICAN GIRLS?>
WELL...
<WE LIKE GIRLS FROM HERE BETTER, AFTER ALL!>

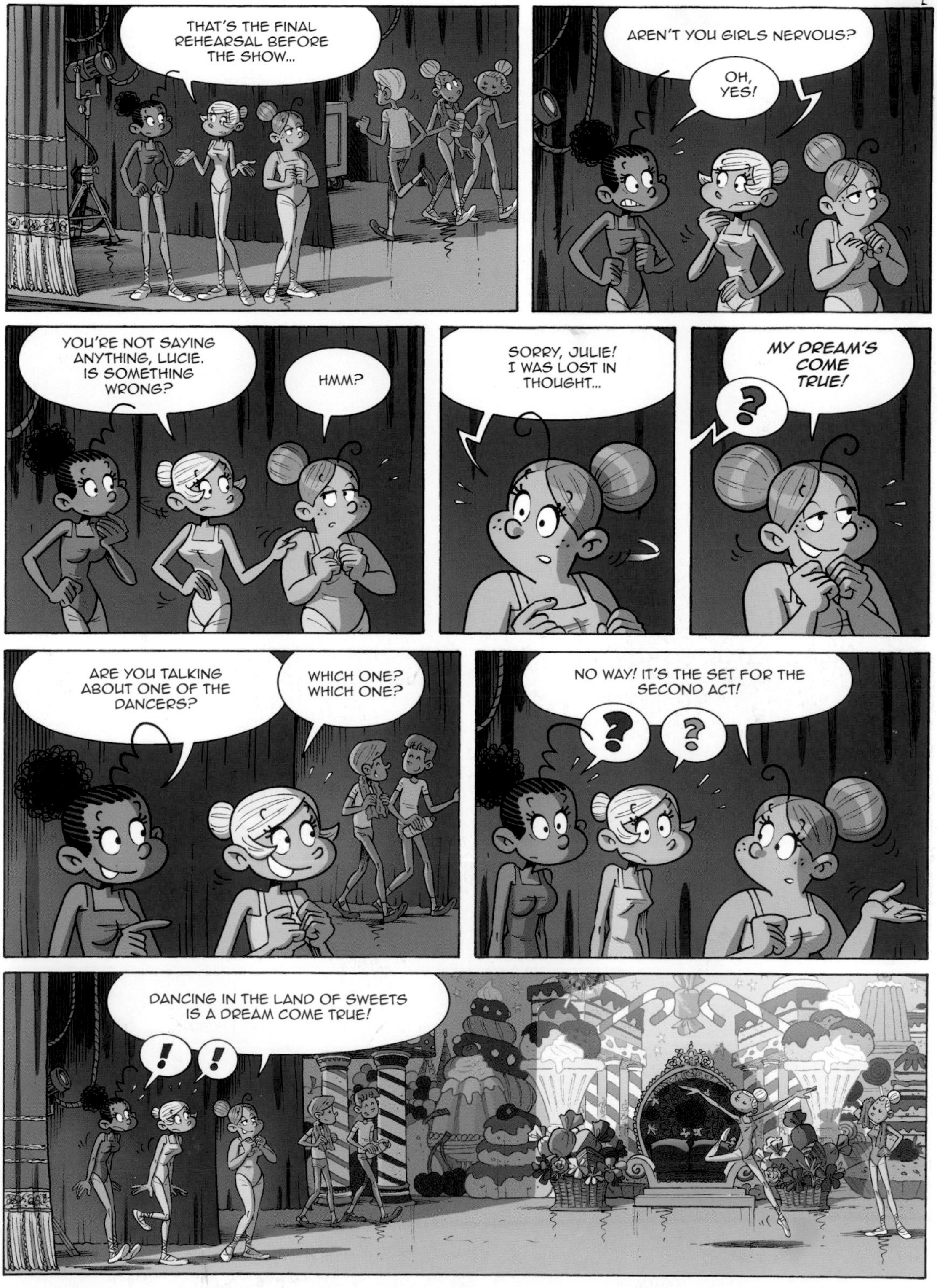
THAT'S THE FINAL REHEARSAL BEFORE THE SHOW...
AREN'T YOU GIRLS NERVOUS?
OH, YES!
YOU'RE NOT SAYING ANYTHING, LUCIE. IS SOMETHING WRONG?
HMM?
SORRY, JULIE! I WAS LOST IN THOUGHT...
?
MY DREAM'S COME TRUE!
ARE YOU TALKING ABOUT ONE OF THE DANCERS?
WHICH ONE? WHICH ONE?
?
?
NO WAY! IT'S THE SET FOR THE SECOND ACT!
!
!
DANCING IN THE LAND OF SWEETS IS A DREAM COME TRUE!

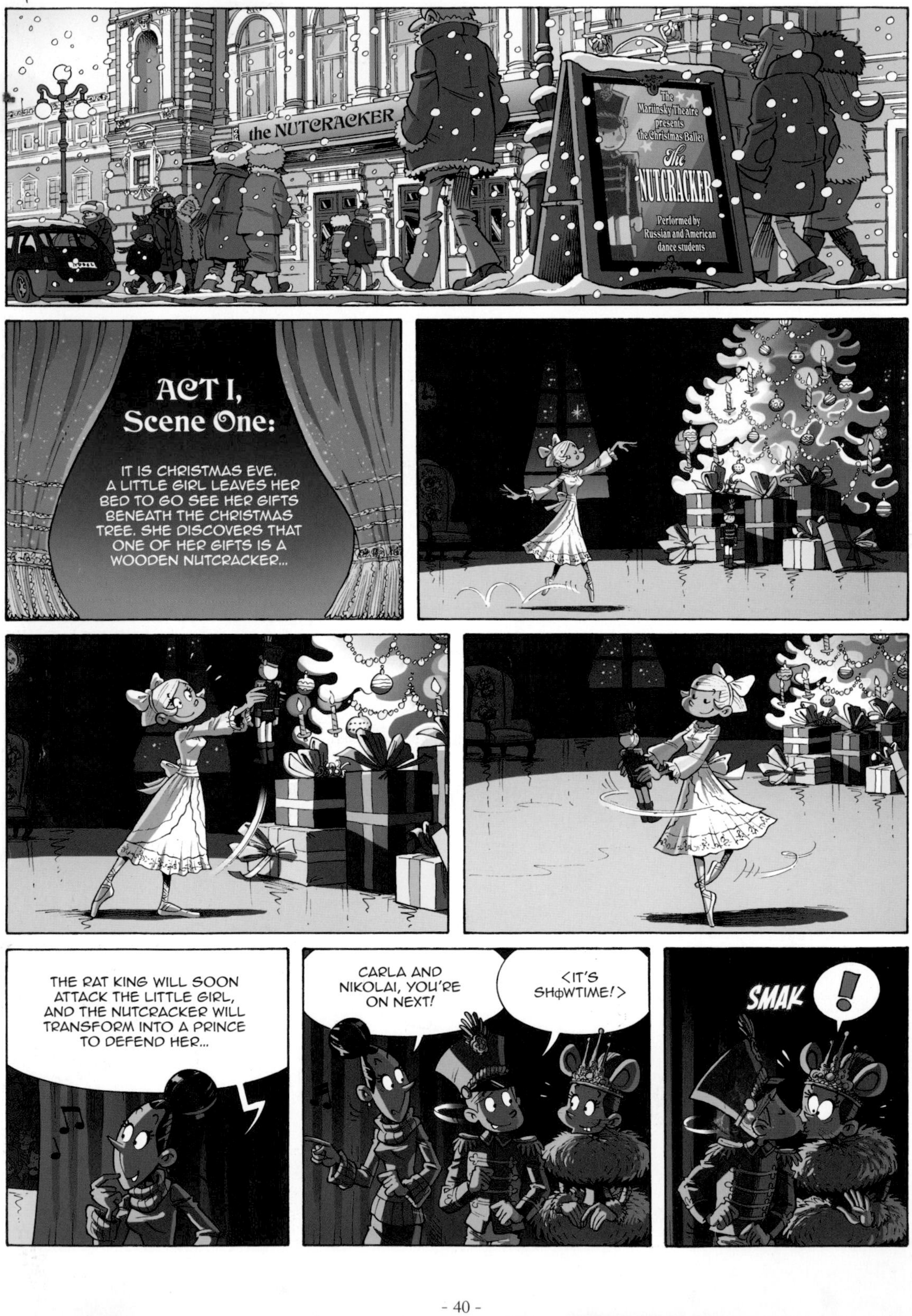
the NUTCRACKER
The Mariinsky Theatre presents the Christmas Ballet
The NUTCRACKER
Performed by Russian and American dance students
ACT I, Scene One:
IT IS CHRISTMAS EVE. A LITTLE GIRL LEAVES HER BED TO GO SEE HER GIFTS BENEATH THE CHRISTMAS TREE. SHE DISCOVERS THAT ONE OF HER GIFTS IS A WOODEN NUTCRACKER...
THE RAT KING WILL SOON ATTACK THE LITTLE GIRL, AND THE NUTCRACKER WILL TRANSFORM INTO A PRINCE TO DEFEND HER...
CARLA AND NIKOLAI, YOU'RE ON NEXT!
<IT'S SHOWTIME!>
SMAK
!

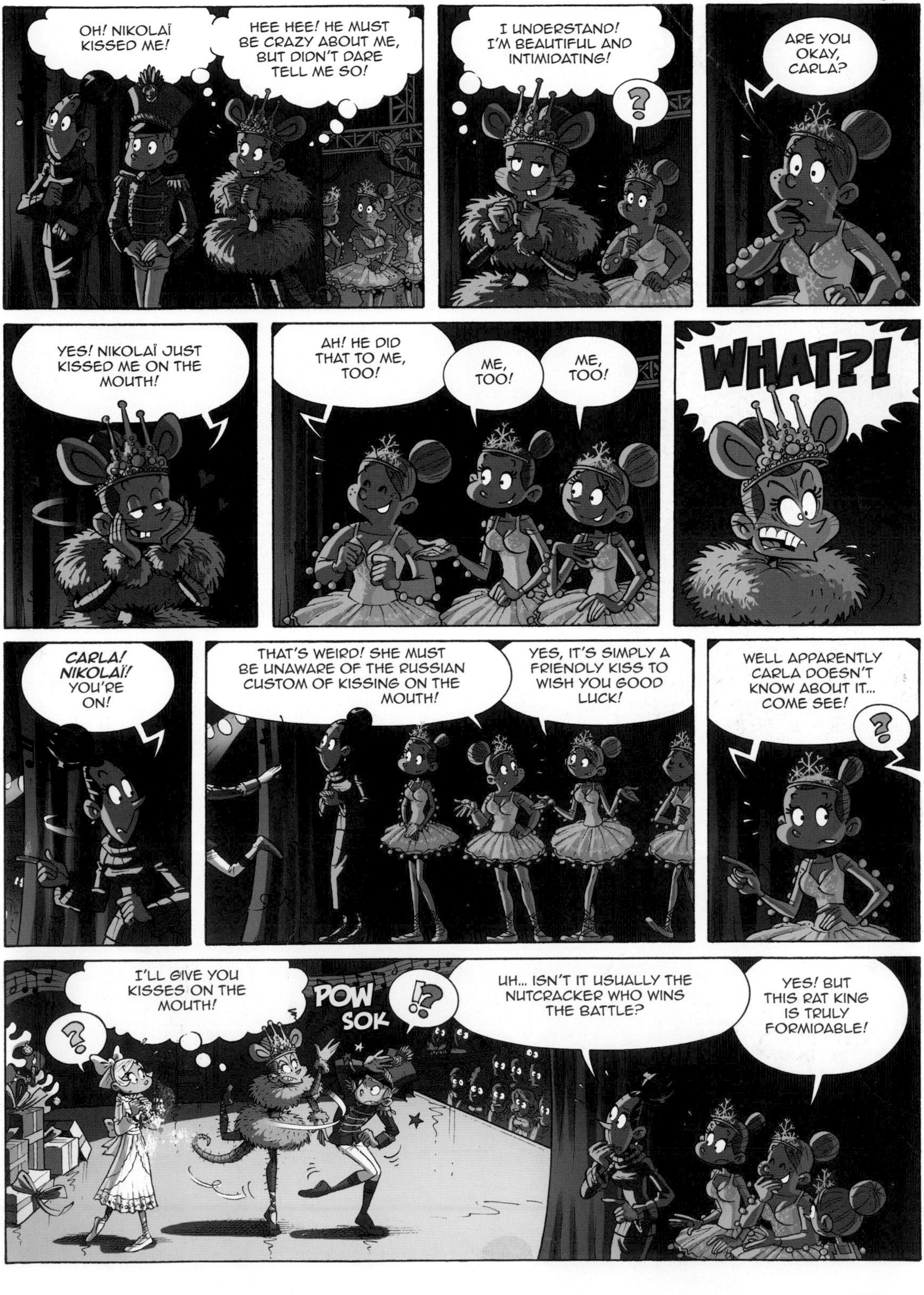
OH! NIKOLAÏ KISSED ME!
HEE HEE! HE MUST BE CRAZY ABOUT ME, BUT DIDN'T DARE TELL ME SO!
I UNDERSTAND! I'M BEAUTIFUL AND INTIMIDATING!
?
ARE YOU OKAY, CARLA?
YES! NIKOLAÏ JUST KISSED ME ON THE MOUTH!
AH! HE DID THAT TO ME, TOO!
ME, TOO!
ME, TOO!
WHAT?!
CARLA! NIKOLAÏ! YOU'RE ON!
THAT'S WEIRD! SHE MUST BE UNAWARE OF THE RUSSIAN CUSTOM OF KISSING ON THE MOUTH!
YES, IT'S SIMPLY A FRIENDLY KISS TO WISH YOU GOOD LUCK!
WELL APPARENTLY CARLA DOESN'T KNOW ABOUT IT... COME SEE!
?
?
I'LL GIVE YOU KISSES ON THE MOUTH!
POW
SOK
!?
UH... ISN'T IT USUALLY THE NUTCRACKER WHO WINS THE BATTLE?
YES! BUT THIS RAT KING IS TRULY FORMIDABLE!

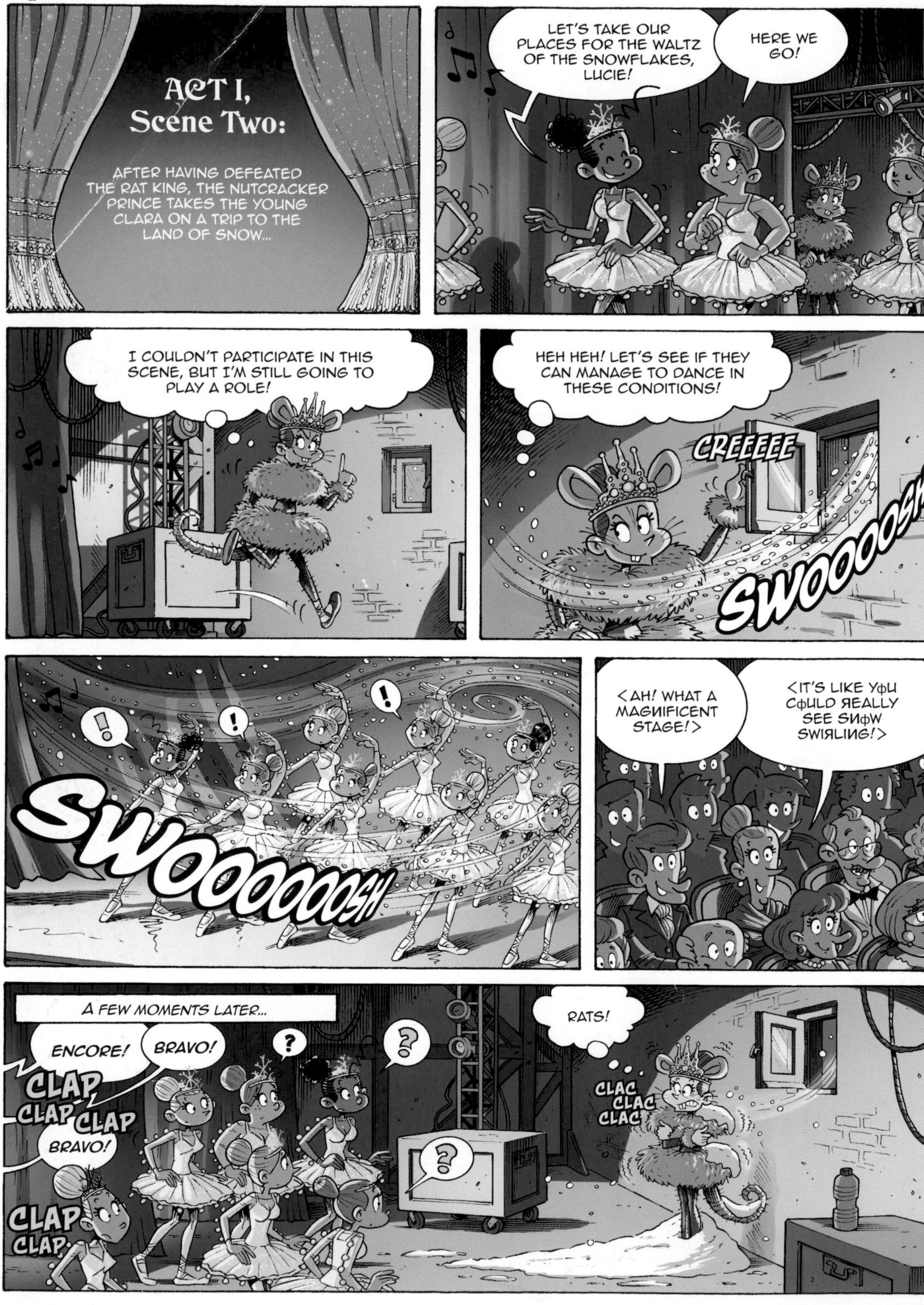
ACT I, Scene Two:
AFTER HAVING DEFEATED THE RAT KING, THE NUTCRACKER PRINCE TAKES THE YOUNG CLARA ON A TRIP TO THE LAND OF SNOW...
LET'S TAKE OUR PLACES FOR THE WALTZ OF THE SNOWFLAKES, LUCIE!
HERE WE GO!
I COULDN'T PARTICIPATE IN THIS SCENE, BUT I'M STILL GOING TO PLAY A ROLE!
HEH HEH! LET'S SEE IF THEY CAN MANAGE TO DANCE IN THESE CONDITIONS!
CREEEEE
SWOOOOSH
!
!
!
SWOOOOOOSH
<AH! WHAT A MAGNIFICENT STAGE!>
<IT'S LIKE YφU CφULD ЯEALLY SEE SNφW SWIЯLING!>
A FEW MOMENTS LATER...
ENCORE!
BRAVO!
?
?
RATS!
CLAP CLAP CLAP
BRAVO!
?
CLAC CLAC CLAC
CLAP CLAP

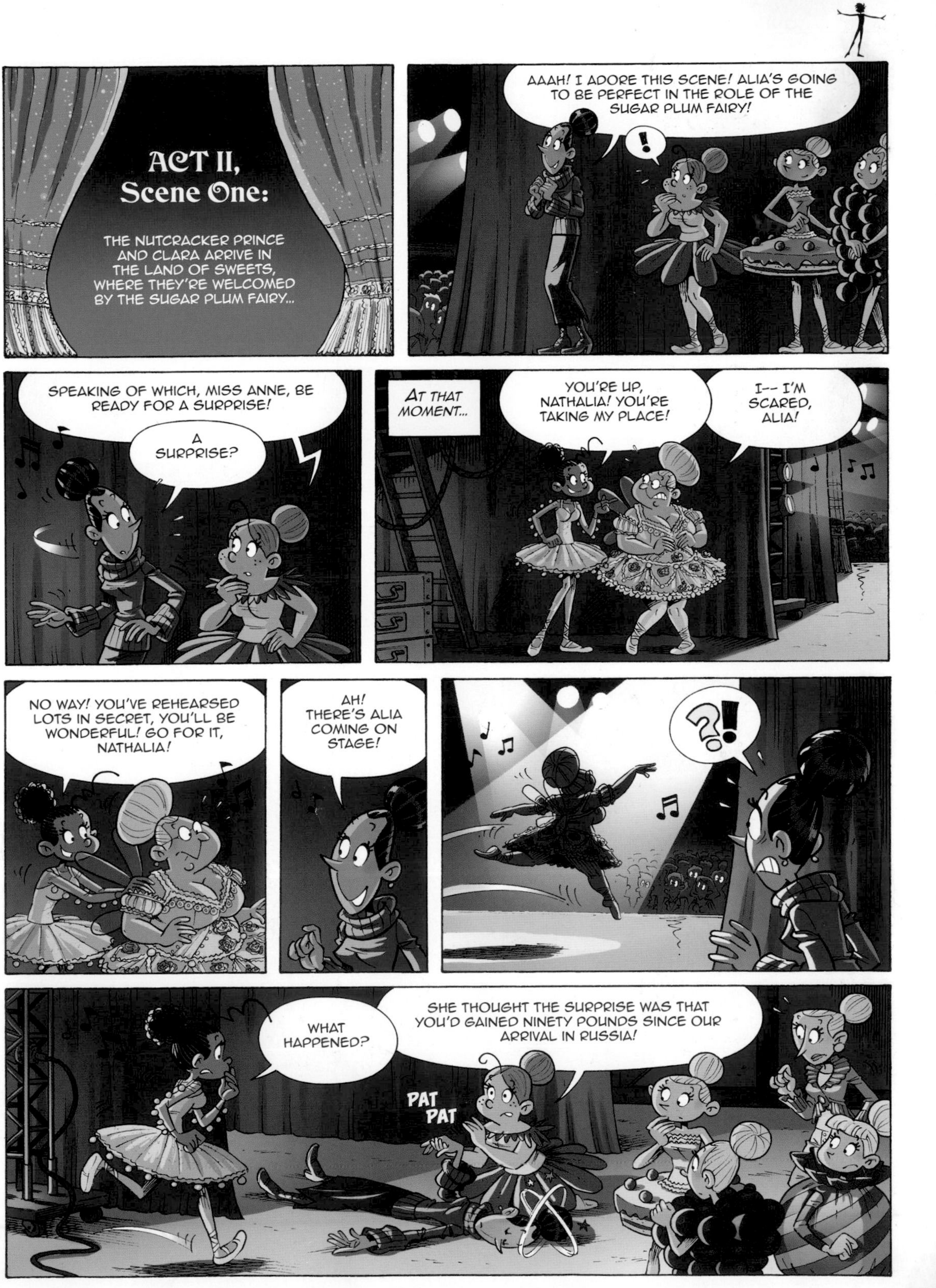
ACT II, Scene One:
THE NUTCRACKER PRINCE AND CLARA ARRIVE IN THE LAND OF SWEETS, WHERE THEY'RE WELCOMED BY THE SUGAR PLUM FAIRY...
AAAH! I ADORE THIS SCENE! ALIA'S GOING TO BE PERFECT IN THE ROLE OF THE SUGAR PLUM FAIRY!
!
SPEAKING OF WHICH, MISS ANNE, BE READY FOR A SURPRISE!
A SURPRISE?
AT THAT MOMENT...
YOU'RE UP, NATHALIA! YOU'RE TAKING MY PLACE!
I-- I'M SCARED, ALIA!
NO WAY! YOU'VE REHEARSED LOTS IN SECRET, YOU'LL BE WONDERFUL! GO FOR IT, NATHALIA!
AH! THERE'S ALIA COMING ON STAGE!
?!
WHAT HAPPENED?
SHE THOUGHT THE SURPRISE WAS THAT YOU'D GAINED NINETY POUNDS SINCE OUR ARRIVAL IN RUSSIA!
PAT PAT

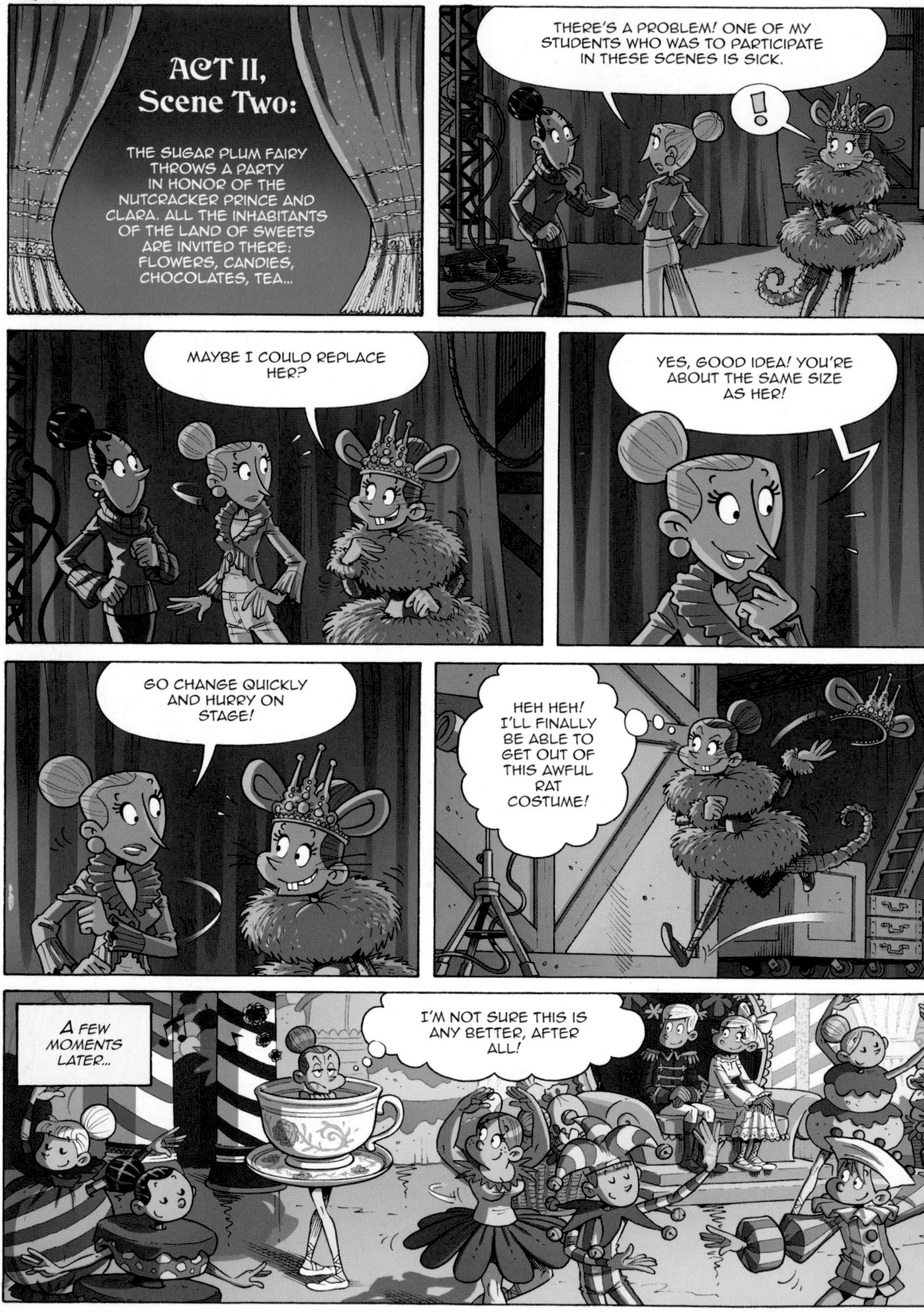

ACT II,
Scene Two:
THE SUGAR PLUM FAIRY THROWS A PARTY IN HONOR OF THE NUTCRACKER PRINCE AND CLARA. ALL THE INHABITANTS OF THE LAND OF SWEETS ARE INVITED THERE: FLOWERS, CANDIES, CHOCOLATES, TEA...
THERE'S A PROBLEM! ONE OF MY STUDENTS WHO WAS TO PARTICIPATE IN THESE SCENES IS SICK.
!
MAYBE I COULD REPLACE HER?
YES, GOOD IDEA! YOU'RE ABOUT THE SAME SIZE AS HER!
GO CHANGE QUICKLY AND HURRY ON STAGE!
HEH HEH! I'LL FINALLY BE ABLE TO GET OUT OF THIS AWFUL RAT COSTUME!
A FEW MOMENTS LATER...
I'M NOT SURE THIS IS ANY BETTER, AFTER ALL!

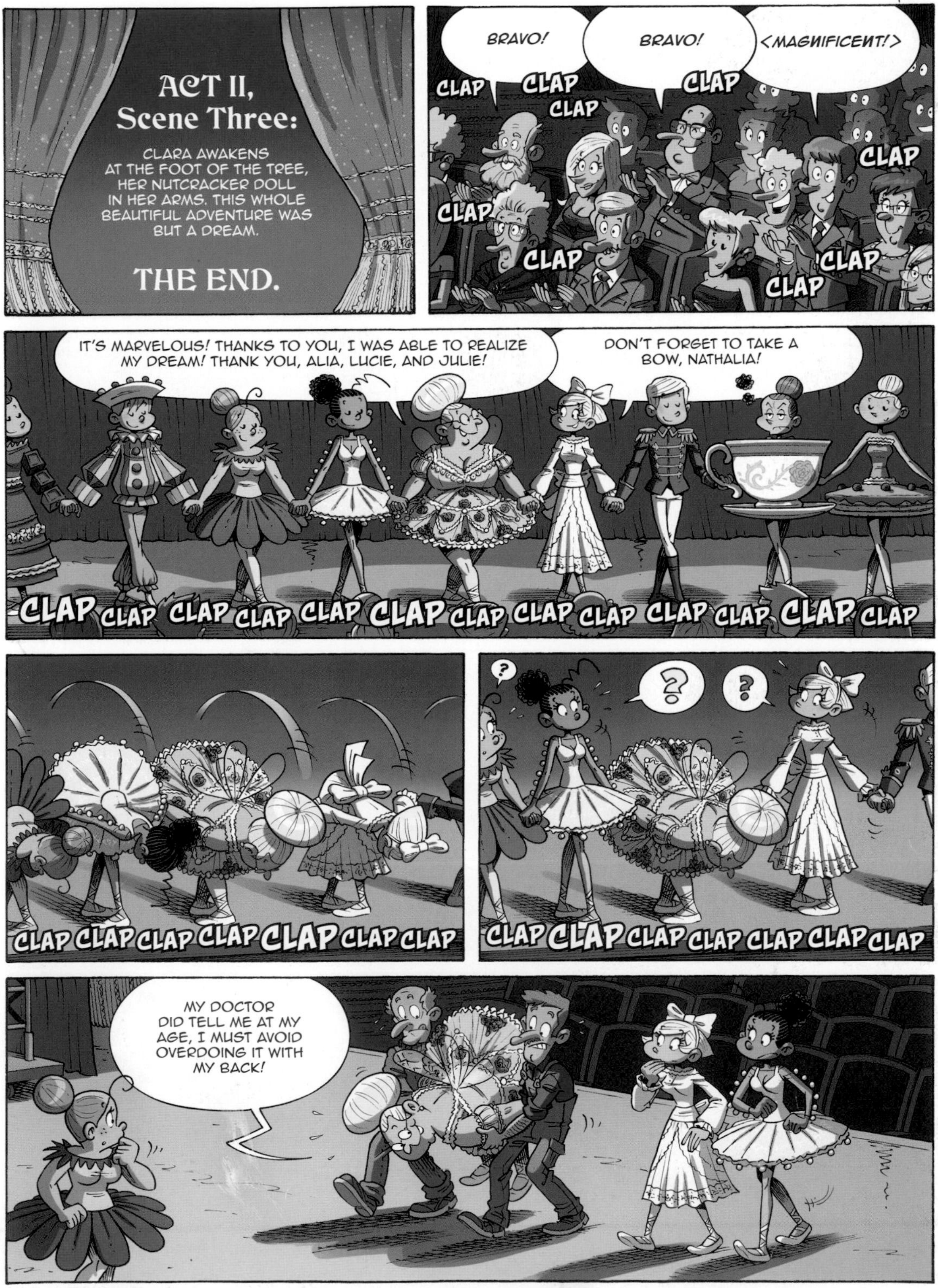

ACT II,
Scene Three:
CLARA AWAKENS AT THE FOOT OF THE TREE, HER NUTCRACKER DOLL IN HER ARMS. THIS WHOLE BEAUTIFUL ADVENTURE WAS BUT A DREAM.
THE END.
BRAVO!
BRAVO!
<MAGNIFICENT!>
CLAP CLAP CLAP CLAP CLAP CLAP CLAP CLAP CLAP
IT'S MARVELOUS! THANKS TO YOU, I WAS ABLE TO REALIZE MY DREAM! THANK YOU, ALIA, LUCIE, AND JULIE!
DON'T FORGET TO TAKE A BOW, NATHALIA!
CLAP CLAP CLAP CLAP CLAP CLAP CLAP CLAP CLAP CLAP CLAP CLAP CLAP
CLAP CLAP CLAP CLAP CLAP CLAP CLAP
?
?
?
CLAP CLAP CLAP CLAP CLAP CLAP CLAP
MY DOCTOR DID TELL ME AT MY AGE, I MUST AVOID OVERDOING IT WITH MY BACK!

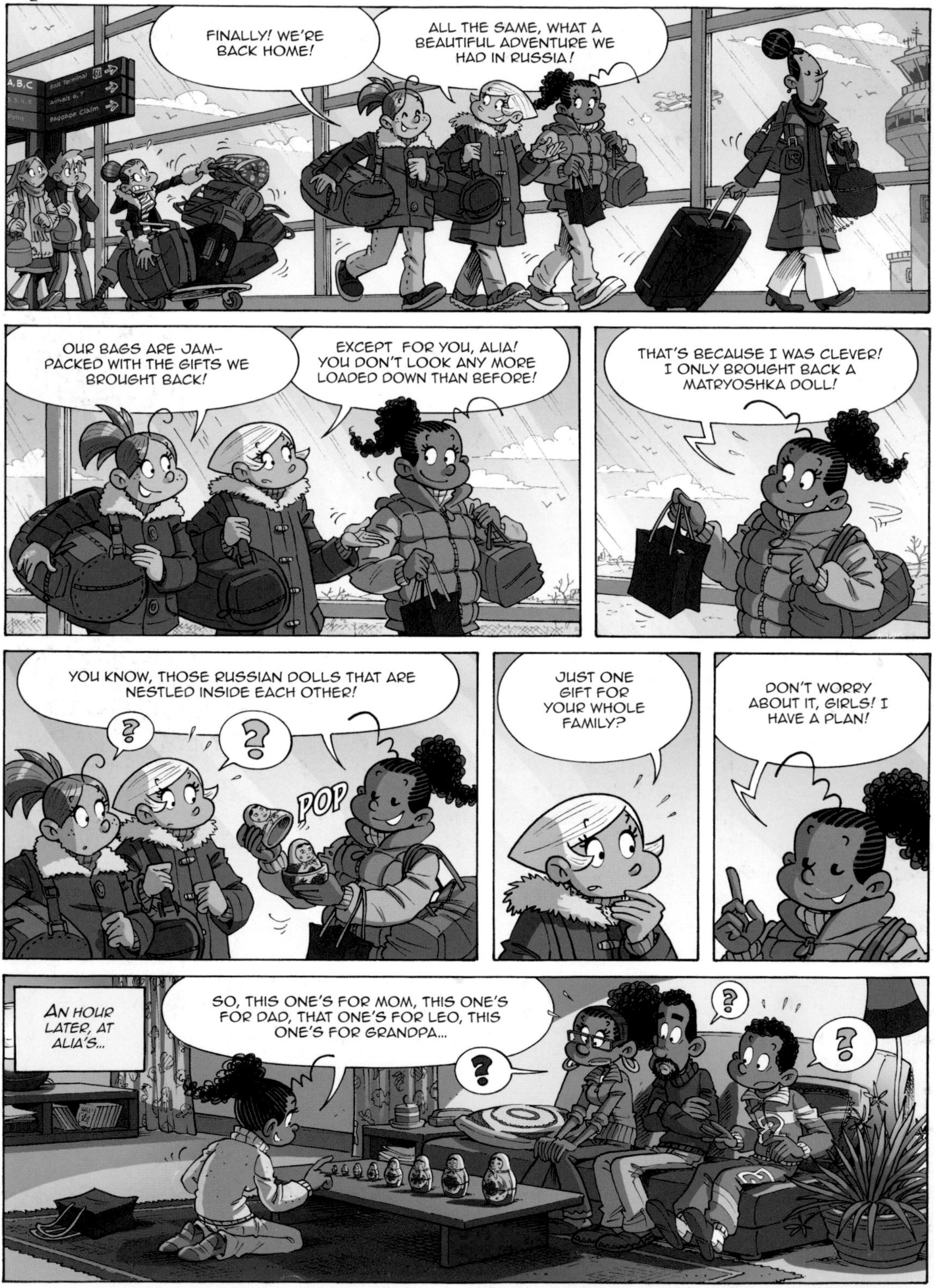
FINALLY! WE'RE BACK HOME!
ALL THE SAME, WHAT A BEAUTIFUL ADVENTURE WE HAD IN RUSSIA!
Baggage Claim
OUR BAGS ARE JAM-PACKED WITH THE GIFTS WE BROUGHT BACK!
EXCEPT FOR YOU, ALIA! YOU DON'T LOOK ANY MORE LOADED DOWN THAN BEFORE!
THAT'S BECAUSE I WAS CLEVER! I ONLY BROUGHT BACK A MATRYOSHKA DOLL!
YOU KNOW, THOSE RUSSIAN DOLLS THAT ARE NESTLED INSIDE EACH OTHER!
?
?
POP
JUST ONE GIFT FOR YOUR WHOLE FAMILY?
DON'T WORRY ABOUT IT, GIRLS! I HAVE A PLAN!
AN HOUR LATER, AT ALIA'S...
SO, THIS ONE'S FOR MOM, THIS ONE'S FOR DAD, THAT ONE'S FOR LEO, THIS ONE'S FOR GRANDPA...
?
?
?

WATCH OUT FOR PAPERCUTZ™

Welcome to the fifth, fancy-footwork-filled DANCE CLASS graphic novel by Crip & Béka. I'm Jim Salicrup, your swing-dancing Editor-in-Chief of Papercutz, the cool cats dedicated to publishing great graphic novels for all ages.

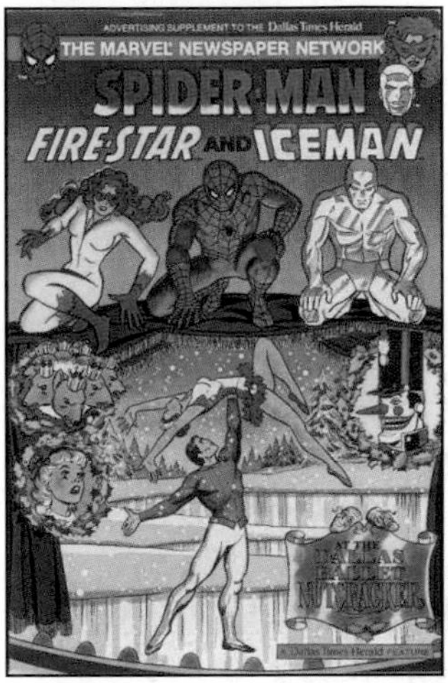
ADVERTISING SUPPLEMENT TO THE Dallas Times Herald
THE MARVEL NEWSPAPER NETWORK
SPIDER-MAN
FIRESTAR AND ICEMAN
Copyright © 1983 Marvel Comics Group.

When I attend dance classes, I often come back to dances I studied years earlier and feel like its brand new and I'm starting all over again. Likewise, it has happened a few times in comics as well. For example, I edited a comic about Pope John Paul II at Marvel Comics, and here at Papercutz we published THE LIFE OF POPE JOHN PAUL II ...*In Comics!*[1] I also once wrote and edited a comicbook that featured Spider-Man and his Amazing Friends, Firestar and Iceman actually attending a performance of *The Nutcracker* ballet. Yes, the comic featured a trio of super-heroes actually watching a ballet from beginning to end without any interruptions from super-villains (that came after)! Now what would be the odds that I would ever edit another comic featuring a performance of *The Nutcracker*? Well, here it is—DANCE CLASS #5 "To Russia, With Love"!

And speaking of Russia, many years ago, one night, after taking a dance class, of course, I met a wonderful young Russian woman named Svetlana Pushkareva, who is also an incredible dancer. From her I learned that what we call "swing" dancing in America, is commonly called "Rock" dancing in Europe. And Svetlana loved swing dancing. While not a professional, I'm sure she could be if she wanted to. One of the places we danced at was "Windows on the World," a restaurant that was on the top floors of the North Tower of the old World Trade Center. I'll never forget how happy she was to see New York City from the windows of that magical place. Another time, Svetlana and her friend, Natasha[2], and I, all went to a swing dance club. At one point, while dancing with Natasha, doing a move called a "throw out," one of us forgot to let go, and I nearly dislocated my shoulder. To this day, I can no longer sleep on my left side. Ah, memories!

And here I am years later at the palatial Papercutz offices, a block away from where the new World Trade Center rises, editing a graphic novel that features *The Nutcracker* ballet, swing dancing, and Russia! I hope they build a restaurant with a dance floor in the top floors of the new Freedom Tower, as there's a friend of mine, who's now a full US citizen, who I would enjoy dancing with there! In the meantime, be sure to keep an eye out for DANCE CLASS #6 "A Merry Olde Christmas" coming soon!

Thanks,

Jim

STAY IN TOUCH!

EMAIL: salicrup@papercutz.com
WEB: www.papercutz.com
TWITTER: @papercutzgn
FACEBOOK: PAPERCUTZGRAPHICNOVELS
MAIL: Papercutz, 160 Broadway,
Suite 700, East Wing, New York, NY 10038

[1]Unfortunately, THE LIFE OF POPE JOHN PAUL II is now out of print from Papercutz.
[2]While it may seem that all Russian women are named either Svetlana or Natasha, it's not true!

More Great Graphic Novels from PAPERCUTZ

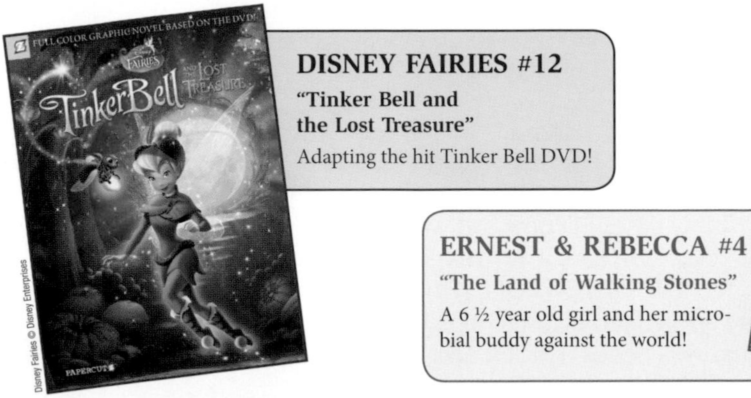

FULL COLOR GRAPHIC NOVEL BASED ON THE DVD!
FAIRIES
TinkerBell and the Lost Treasure
PAPERCUTZ

DISNEY FAIRIES #12
"Tinker Bell and the Lost Treasure"
Adapting the hit Tinker Bell DVD!

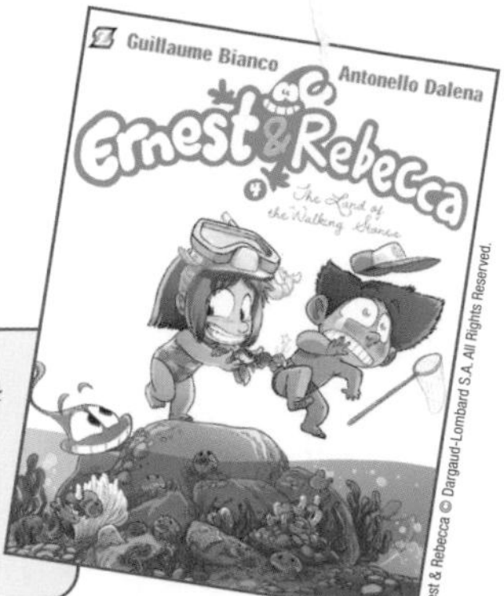

Guillaume Bianco
Antonello Dalena
Ernest & Rebecca
The Land of the Walking Stones

ERNEST & REBECCA #4
"The Land of Walking Stones"
A 6 ½ year old girl and her microbial buddy against the world!

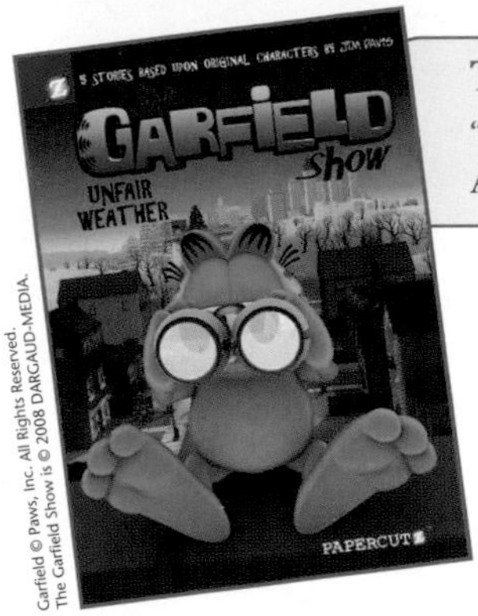

GARFIELD Show
UNFAIR WEATHER
PAPERCUTZ

THE GARFIELD SHOW #1
"Unfair Weather"
As seen on the Cartoon Network!

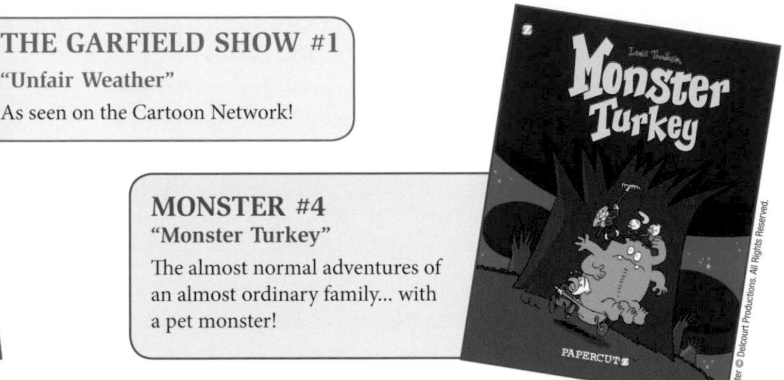

Monster Turkey
PAPERCUTZ

MONSTER #4
"Monster Turkey"
The almost normal adventures of an almost ordinary family... with a pet monster!

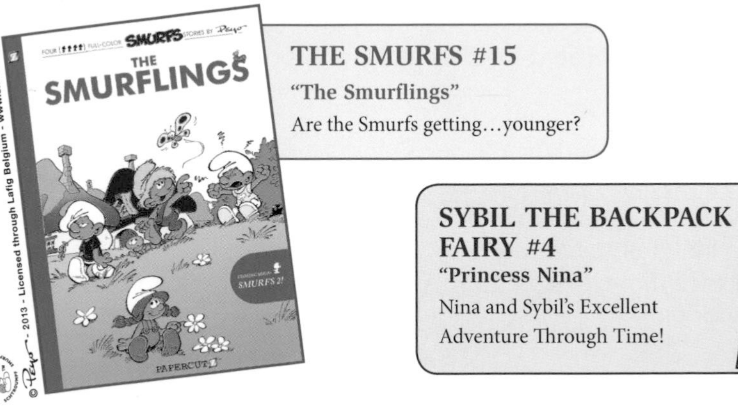

SMURFS
THE SMURFLINGS
SMURFS 2!
PAPERCUTZ

THE SMURFS #15
"The Smurflings"
Are the Smurfs getting...younger?

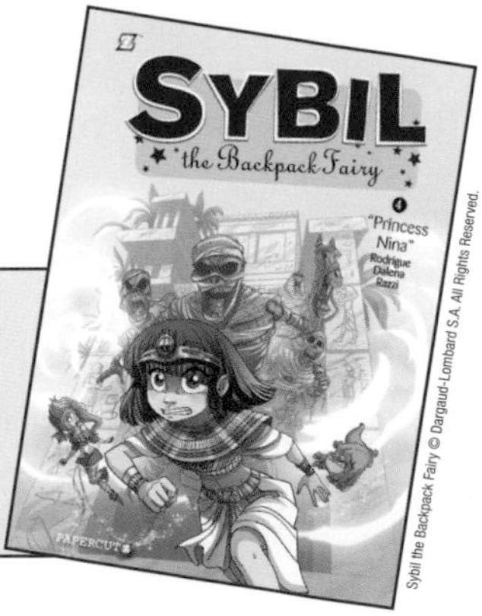

SYBIL
the Backpack Fairy
4
"Princess Nina"
PAPERCUTZ

SYBIL THE BACKPACK FAIRY #4
"Princess Nina"
Nina and Sybil's Excellent Adventure Through Time!

Available at better booksellers everywhere!

Or order directly from us! DISNEY FAIRIES is available in paperback for $7.99, in hardcover for $11.99; ERNEST & REBECCA is $11.99 in hardcover only; THE GARFIELD SHOW is available in paperback for $7.99, in hardcover for $11.99; MONSTER is available in hardcover only for $9.99; THE SMURFS are available in paperback for $5.99, in hardcover for $10.99; and SYBIL THE BACKPACK FAIRY is available in hardcover only for $10.99.

Please add $4.00 for postage and handling for the first book, add $1.00 for each additional book.

Please make check payable to NBM Publishing Send to: PAPERCUTZ, 160 Broadway, Suite 700, East Wing, New York, NY 10038 (1-800-886-1223)

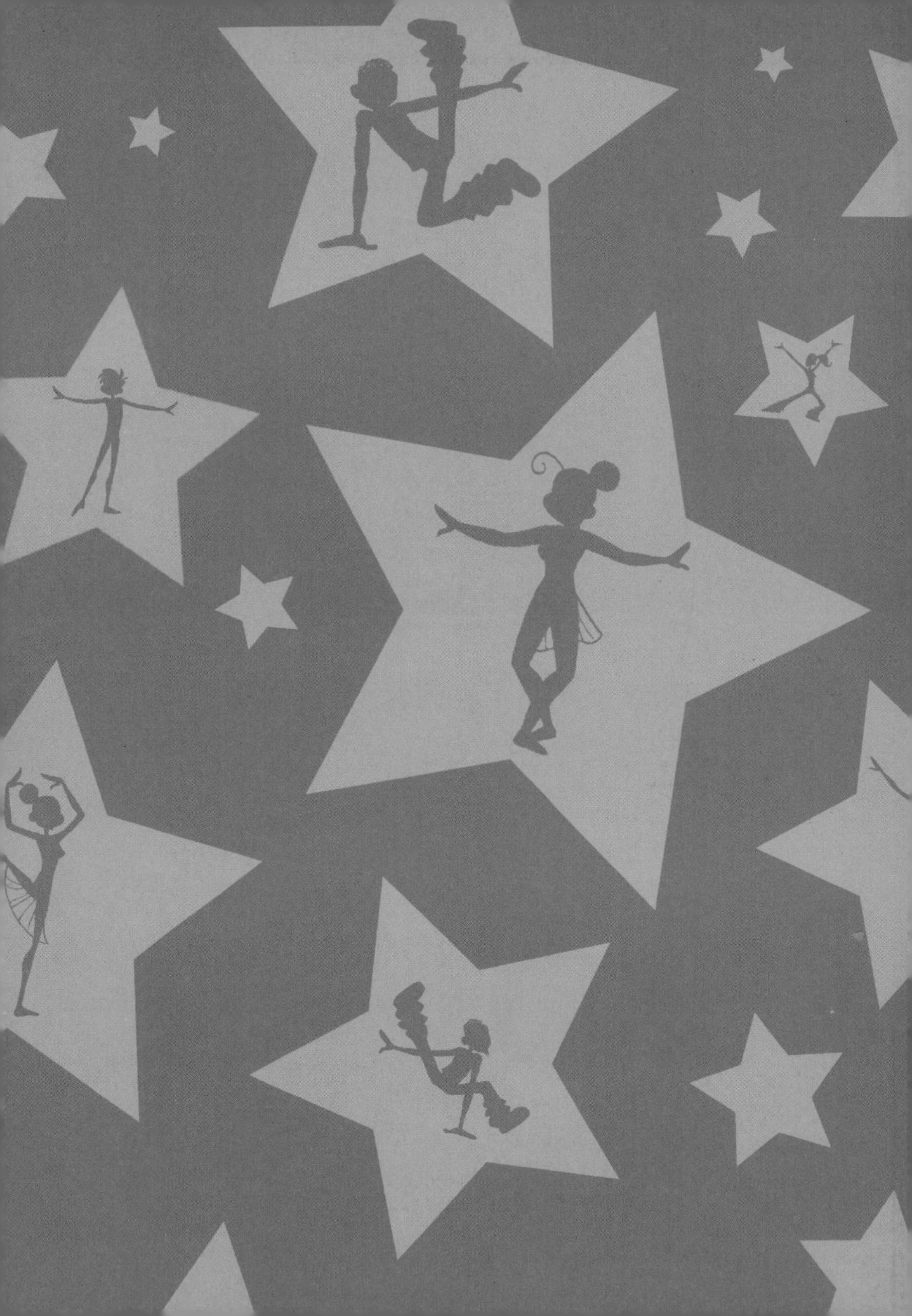